WA...
A RICHARD DONNER...
A JOEL SCHUMACHER *Film*
· THE LOST BOYS ·
COREY FELDMAN · JAMI GERTZ
COREY HAIM · EDWARD HERRMANN
BARNARD HUGHES · JASON PATRIC
KIEFER SUTHERLAND *and* DIANNE WIEST
Music by THOMAS NEWMAN
Director of Photography MICHAEL CHAPMAN
Executive Producer RICHARD DONNER
Story by JANICE FISCHER & JAMES JEREMIAS
Screenplay by JANICE FISCHER &
JAMES JEREMIAS *and* JEFFREY BOAM
Produced by HARVEY BERNHARD
Directed by JOEL SCHUMACHER

PANAVISION®

IN SELECTED THEATRES

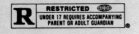

R RESTRICTED
UNDER 17 REQUIRES ACCOMPANYING
PARENT OR ADULT GUARDIAN

WARNER BROS.
A WARNER COMMUNICATIONS COMPANY
©1987 Warner Bros. Inc. All Rights Reserved

THE
LOST·BOYS

A novel by Craig Shaw Gardner
Based on a screenplay by Janice Fischer
& James Jeremias and Jeffrey Boam
Story by Janice Fischer & James Jeremias

BERKLEY BOOKS, NEW YORK

THE LOST BOYS

A Berkley Book/published by arrangement with
Warner Bros. Inc.

PRINTING HISTORY
Berkley edition/August 1987

All rights reserved.
Copyright © 1987 by Warner Bros. Inc.
This book may not be reproduced in whole or in part,
by mimeograph or any other means, without permission.
For information address: The Berkley Publishing Group,
200 Madison Avenue, New York, New York 10016.

ISBN: 0-425-10044-8

A BERKLEY BOOK® TM 757,375
Berkley Books are published by The Berkley Publishing Group,
200 Madison Avenue, New York, New York 10016.
The name "BERKLEY" and the "B" logo are trademarks
belonging to Berkley Publishing Corporation.

PRINTED IN THE UNITED STATES OF AMERICA

10   9   8   7   6   5   4   3   2   1

Prologue

Let me tell you about Santa Carla.

It's right out there on the Pacific. You can stand out on the beach at night and look at the surf breaking in the moonlight and swear that it's one of the most beautiful places on this earth. On summer nights the kids—and there's a lot of kids in Santa Carla—build bonfires on the beach, a strip of leaping orange and yellow lights as far as the eye can see. That's pretty, too, as long as the kids aren't being too rowdy that particular night.

That's one problem with Santa Carla; the town isn't really big on peace and quiet. In fact, turn around, away from the beach and the beautiful view, and you'll see the cause of all that racket, the real center of town.

The Boardwalk.

That's right. There it is, all that music and all that noise, the beating heart of Santa Carla. You can walk up there, past the three-tries-for-a-dollar booths with the hucksters urging you to win a big teddy bear for the little lady, past the food stands where the kids can load up on hot dogs and cotton candy, past the Tilt-a-Whirl, the Giant Mouse, and the Snake, where the kids have a chance to lose what they just ate, up past the giant Ferris wheel, so brightly lit that it takes the place of the stars in the nighttime sky. Then you come to the carousel. The kids call it a "merry-go-round," but what do they know? You want to learn something else about Santa Carla, that's the next place you go.

Besides, that's where the whole story started, right inside there.

It's a nice carousel. Real, carved wooden horses, and a calliope that plays old-fashioned songs, the type some old fogies I know would call "the kind they don't write any-more." Of course, they probably never wrote piano rolls for "Sunshine of Your Love" or "Boogie Oogie Oogie," and the kids don't seem to mind. Somehow, when you're riding up and down on a wooden horse, you want to hear how Casey would waltz with a strawberry blond. Know what I mean?

This particular night, there was a certain bunch of kids riding the carousel. You'd recognize this bunch anywhere around Santa Carla, if not from their Mohawks and shaved heads and "punk" tattoos, then from the way they dressed. You know, their Day-Glo T-shirts with "My Beach, My Wave" scrawled across the chests, and their wet suits and surfing tank tops. This is one of the big gangs around Santa Carla.

They call themselves the "Surf Nazis." Charming name, don't you think?

Well, they laughed and jumped around the moving car-ousel, jostling the other riders, letting all the kids know that their gang owned this ride. Their leader, Greg, just leaned back on one of the carousel's benches and watched it all, a half smile on his face, his arm around Shelly, his girl. The calliope started to play "Waltzing Matilda."

And then the Lost Boys walked in. Another gang, a lot better dressed than the Surf Nazis, but still a gang. Their leader, a tall, blond fellow named David, walked up and got right on the slowly moving carousel. The ride was almost over. The other Lost Boys followed him on. And as they spun around, Shelly managed to smile in David's direction.

David smiled back and nodded his head slightly in greet-ing, a polite gesture, the sort of friendly nod you might see a hundred times in the course of a day.

Greg didn't think so. He scowled at his girlfriend and

jumped up from his seat. He took a couple steps in the Boys' direction, but the other gang was moving too. No, not to face Greg. He realized they were going to go by him as if he weren't even there.

Greg stood up and said something that wasn't exactly flattering. He shoved the Lost Boy out of the way.

But now David was there. The calliope played on. *Waltzing Matilda*. The Surf Nazis joined Greg. *Waltzing Matilda*. The Lost Boys closed ranks as well. If the Surf Nazis wanted a fight, they were ready. *Won't you go a-waltzing, Matilda, with me*.

Greg stared at David. David took a half step forward.

He found a nightstick pressed against his Adam's apple. David let his eyes follow the nightstick down to a beefy hand, attached to the body of Big Ed. All three hundred pounds of Big Ed, a security guard with no love for Surf Nazis or Lost Boys.

The carousel ground to a halt. The music stopped. The ride was over.

Big Ed's mouth was small for his head. When he opened it, his voice was soft after the calliope's "Waltzing Matilda."

"I told you to stay off the Boardwalk."

David stared at the guard, not moving for a long moment. Big Ed's eyes were small, too, but the anger there made up for what they lacked in size.

David smiled and turned his head toward the Lost Boys.

"Come on," he said to the others, "let's pull."

He walked away, and the Lost Boys followed. Big Ed turned to the others.

"You too," he barked in Greg's face. "Off the Boardwalk. And don't come back!"

Greg stared at the guard, looking for a moment as if he might spit in Big Ed's face. He turned away instead and walked slowly toward the door, with the other gang members following. He waited until he was out of Big Ed's hearing before he mumbled something that made the other Surf Nazis laugh. Then they, too, left the carousel house.

It was getting late. Time to shut down the hot dog booths, the three-for-a-dollar come-ons, the Tilt-a-Whirl, the Ferris wheel, and the Giant Mouse. Big Ed watched the banks of lights go out one by one as the amusement park closed down for the night.

Damn those gangs! Ed cursed them all as he opened his locker and retrieved his lunch pail. None of those kids were any good! Not that Ed hated kids. He had a couple of his own, after all. It was those gangs, that was it.

He knew how to handle those gangs. If only they'd let him carry a gun. Shoot through a couple of those snot-nosed Surf Nazis and you'd be surprised how fast the rest of them would disappear. That would be the end of your gang problem on the Boardwalk.

But he'd never get a gun, just like he'd never be able to pass the police exam. Life just wasn't fair, that was all. Lunch pail in hand, Big Ed slammed his locker closed and headed for the parking lot.

Three in the morning and it was almost quiet in Santa Carla. The only sounds were Big Ed's boots crunching on the gravel as he walked the length of the empty parking lot to reach his car, and the soft grumble of his voice as he cursed out all the kids who parked here in the evening so that he had to leave his car way out here. The last thing he wanted to do was take a walk like this at three A.M. He needed to get some sleep. Damn all these kids, anyways!

Big Ed heard another noise. At first he thought it was the wind, rushing in suddenly off the beach. But he heard something else too. There were other sounds behind the wind, a high, screeching sound, like chalk skittering across a blackboard, and a whispering, like a hundred voices softly calling his name.

Big Ed looked up. His eyes widened with surprise. He opened his mouth to scream.

Before he could scream, he was gone. His lunch pail clattered across the worn pavement, the only sign that the three-hundred-pound security guard had ever crossed this parking lot.

I know just what you'll say next. Where could he go? A man of that size just can't disappear. And yet the only faces you would see on the Boardwalk just then were the painted ones that leer from the sides fo the fun house. The beach was deserted too. All the bonfires had gone out. The only sound left was the lapping of the waves.

But then, on the beach, there was another noise. A rush of wind, a screeching, a whispering. Something fell with a thud into the wet sand.

If it wasn't for the uniform, you wouldn't know that this pitiful thing on the beach had anything in common with Big Ed. What had once been a beefy security guard was now nothing but a rag doll, nothing left beneath his clothes but bones and skin. There was a big hole in his neck, the flesh ripped clean away. Only a few bits of tattered meat still clung to the bone.

But it wasn't a messy corpse. Not really. It was all dried out. All the blood was gone. Every drop.

Big Ed's lifeless eyes stared into the sky as the wind and whispering faded into the night.

It was quiet at last in Santa Carla.

One

"Santa Carla, here we come!" his mother shouted for perhaps the tenth time. Her short red hair blew back from her face as she turned her head around, trying to get her son to share her enthusiasm.

But the thought of Santa Carla didn't make Michael Emerson the least bit excited. He slumped in the backseat and stared halfheartedly out the window at the sky. Maybe, he thought, he should sit up and take a look at the coastline flying by. His younger brother, Sam, was sitting up front with his designer clothes and designer hair, perfectly happy sharing the front passenger seat with their dog, Nanook. Both dog and Sam sat with their heads out the window, watching the world go by.

Michael knew he should look too. There might be someplace he could take his motorcycle, maybe even someplace out of the way he could show to a girl. Somehow, though, he didn't even have the energy to sit up. He didn't really care. That was it. Right now he really didn't care about much of anything.

His life was over. That was it. No matter what his mother said about moving on and finding new adventures, he felt like he'd left his life behind him in Phoenix. All his friends were there. He'd been doing all right in school. And there was Laurie. They weren't really close yet, had only gone out together a couple times. Somehow, though, being with Laurie had been special, so much different from any of the other girls he had dated. When he had thought of taking a girl out on his bike a moment before, he realized he had thought of Laurie.

Now she was gone, part of a life Michael would never see again. Why did his mother and father have to go through their divorce? Oh, realistically, Michael knew. He had been there for all the fights, after all, had seen his father disappear for two weeks without a word, had sat with his mother all those nights that she could do nothing but cry. But why did they have to move away?

Michael knew that too. His mother had explained it to him until he had practically memorized the words. Even after their little scandal his father was still a pretty important person in their part of town. There was no way they could stay in Phoenix without running into him. He didn't want the kids, and Mom didn't want him. So Michael and Mom were on their way to Santa Carla, along with brother Sam, dog Nanook, and all their worldly goods.

Their grandfather lived in Santa Carla. From now on they would stay with him. That was fine with his mother, Michael guessed. And his brother was happy as long as he could buy his comic books and watch his brat-pack movies. Michael sighed and sank lower into his seat. Was he ever going to find anyplace that he really belonged?

The car groaned as it started up another incline. Michael glanced back at the U-Haul trailer they dragged behind them. This old Land Rover of their mother's could barely take the extra weight. "Santa Carla, here we come!" his mother kept shouting. With the way this broken-down bus was acting, "Santa Carla or bust!" was more like it.

They drove by a group of stores his mother seemed to recognize: a convenience store, a beauty salon, a post office that needed a coat of paint. "We're getting close!" she called over her shoulder.

Sam frowned and leaned toward the window. "What's that smell?"

Their mother laughed and took a deep breath. "Ocean air!" she proclaimed.

"Smells like something died," Sam replied, looking slightly nauseated.

Their mother threw her hands up in the air, then quickly placed them back on the steering wheel.

"Guys," she began slowly, "I know the last year hasn't been easy, but I think you're really going to like living in Santa Carla!"

Sam glanced back at his brother. He still looked slightly nauseated. Michael shrugged hopelessly. He sat up enough to look out the window.

Their mother paused for a minute, waiting for a response.

"How about some music?" she asked at last. She reached over and turned on the radio. Steel guitar whined from the speaker while a deep male voice lamented how he'd lost his wife because of whiskey.

Sam turned back to her.

"Keep going," he instructed.

She turned the dial. The Thousand and One Strings played a Paul McCartney song.

"Keep going!" Sam insisted even more urgently.

Their mother turned the dial again. The Young Rascals sang about sitting around on summer afternoons.

"Keep going!" Sam and Michael shouted in unison.

Their mother laughed. "Wait a moment! This one's from my era!" She began to sing along.

"Groooovin'!"

Sam looked back at Michael again. Michael knew what he was thinking. What was this nonsense? What did you do when you were 'groovin',' anyway?

They turned back to their mother.

"Keep going!" This time their voices held a hint of desperation.

The three of them laughed as their mother twisted the dial again, finding a decent rock and roll station at last.

Guitar and drums, a song about being on the highway. Michael sat up in the backseat and smiled despite himself, gently hitting his leg in time to the radio. Now this was music!

"Here we are!" his mother prompted.

Michael looked up to see them rapidly approaching a huge billboard. On one edge of the large blue sign was a jumping swordfish, on the other a bikini-clad girl with a beach ball. Between the two were the words: WELCOME TO SANTA CARLA.

So they were finally here. Michael kept watching the billboard as if those four words and the pictures surrounding them would give him some clue about his new home, as if they would speak up and tell him just what he should do to settle into this new town: how to make friends, how to fit in, how to be happy and forget about other people in other places.

Michael stared at the sign until the Land Rover passed it by, then turned to look out the back window at the sign's other side. Somebody had spray-painted something in red across the billboard's rear. It took Michael a moment to make out the words: MURDER CAPITAL OF THE WORLD.

"What?" Michael turned back to his mother and brother, but they were both facing forward. He was the only one who had seen the sign. Sam pointed at a brightly colored storefront. His mother laughed.

Michael looked out the back window again, but the sign had disappeared with distance.

Welcome to Santa Carla.

Murder Capital of the World?

Two

Lucy Emerson watched two small girls bouncing on the trampolines. Up, down, up, down. It certainly was busy here. Santa Carla was a real, old-fashioned summer resort, full of flashing signs and moving bodies. In the last five blocks they had passed pizza joints, surfers, bikini shops, bikers, ice-cream parlors, and about two miles' worth of "beach parking," which got a dollar more expensive with every block that they got closer to the beach. And when they needed gas, they had pulled into a self-service gas station that also managed to rent surfboards, and had a trampoline ride on the side. Whatever brought in the money, Lucy supposed.

That's something else they were going to need in the near future: money. She watched the electronic numbers multiply on the gas pump as Michael filled their gas tank and imagined what little money she still had flying from her purse to vanish in thin air. She shook her head. She was being silly. A Land Rover certainly wasn't the most economical vehicle for gas mileage. Still, it had gotten them to Santa Carla in one piece. She worried too much. Now that they were about to start a new life, she should concentrate on the good things for a while.

Somehow, though, the bad things kept coming back to haunt her. Her friends said it was natural; her divorce had just been finalized, after all. It was a divorce she'd rather forget about, too; every messy little detail. Once Lance had done those things to her, she never even wanted to think about him again, either. Her friends had all said she had let him off easy. She supposed she had. She certainly could have gotten more money than the minimal child support the judge had awarded her. But all she really wanted was for the divorce to be over and done with. It was too painful any other way.

She worried, sometimes, about taking the boys away from their father. Not for their father's sake—oh, no. She didn't think she'd ever have a kind thought for that man again. But should teenage boys be left without a man they could look up to?

Well, there was her father, of course. Now that the boys were going to live with their grandfather, she supposed he could take over some of the responsibilities of role model. Then again, with the way her father had been acting lately, she wondered if the boys might make a better role model for him than the other way around.

"All set, Mom!" Michael called from the back of the Land Rover. Lucy glanced a final time at the numbers on the pump and handed the attendant a twenty.

Sam came running up, Nanook barking at his heels.

"Mom!" Sam managed, despite being out of breath. "There's an amusement park right on the beach!"

Lucy smiled. Sam wasn't going to have any trouble adjusting at all.

"That's the Boardwalk, Sam."

Sam's eyes lit up as if the name were magic. "Boardwalk? Can we go, Mom?"

Lucy brushed at her son's hair. "Maybe later. Grandpa's expecting us."

Her eyes wandered back to the trampolines. The two little girls were gone, but there were two other teenagers in the corner of the lot by the dumpster. Their eyes followed the attendant as he walked into the office to fetch Lucy's change. The minute he disappeared, they had flipped the top from the bin and eagerly rummaged through the garbage. Lucy realized they must be looking for food. The two of them were so thin! Their clothes were threadbare as well. One of them had worn a hole in the elbow of his sweatshirt. Could boys like this live around here?

"Here you are, ma'am."

Lucy turned back to see the attendant holding a five-dollar bill in her direction. She took it and looked back to the runaways. The attendant looked there as well.

"Hey!" he called out, suddenly angry. "What'd I tell you kids? Get away from there!"

Reluctantly, the boys backed away from the dumpster. Grumbling, the attendant walked back to the office, his eyes never leaving the runaways.

"Sam." Lucy handed the five dollar bill to her son and pointed to the emaciated teenagers. "Tell them to get something to eat."

Sam stared at the money in his hand. "I thought we were poor."

Lucy smiled and shook her head. "Not that poor. Go on, now."

Sam chased after the runaways. Lucy started back toward the driver's seat. She saw Michael standing by the office door, talking to the attendant. Michael asked the attendant if he knew of any jobs around.

"Nothing legal," was the attendant's response.

Michael thanked the older man and trotted back toward the U-Haul. He nodded to his mother.

"This is where I get off."

He jumped on the trailer and quickly untied a pair of ropes to free his motorbike, then retied the ropes to secure the rest of their belongings. It was amazing, Lucy thought, how efficient her son could be when he really wanted to be. He lowered the trailer's sliding ramp to the ground and walked the bike down to the pavement.

"Still mad at me?" Lucy asked.

"For what?" Michael replied. He wiped his shaggy

brown hair from his eyes and looked up from his most prized possession.

Lucy shrugged. "For everything."

Michael frowned and got on his bike. Lucy was immediately sorry she had said anything. Her son was only a teenager, after all. He put up a brave front, but he had a lot of trouble dealing with his emotions. And Lucy was sure that this whole divorce thing hadn't made it any easier on him.

"Michael?" she added before her son could leave. "If you want some time on your own, you can meet us later. It's okay."

Sam chose this moment to return, his sneakers pumping across the asphalt.

"What?" Sam somehow managed to sound mortally wounded. "He *can* and I *can't*? No fair!"

Oh, dear. Lucy could feel a fight brewing. Sibling rivalry rears its ugly head. How was she going to get out of this one?

"That's okay, Mom." Michael shook his head. "I'll follow you and help you unload."

Lucy smiled. Wonderful, wonderful Michael! He was more responsible than she gave him credit for. She wondered what she should say to him, to let him know how much his helping out meant to her. Michael smiled at her for a second, then glanced down at his bike. She decided to say nothing at all. She would end up embarrassing him all over again.

"Come on, Sam," she said instead. "Let's get in the car."

She opened the door on the driver's side as Sam pushed in again next to Nanook. She saw someone wave as she climbed into the driver's seat. She looked up to see the two skinny teenagers. One of them clutched the five-dollar bill in a grimy hand.

"Hey, thanks, lady!" he called.

"Use some of it to call home!" she shouted back. This just went to show her, she thought. She should be content that her two boys were still with her, both of them reasonably happy and well dressed.

Sam frowned as he glanced in the rearview mirror, running a hand through his very recently cut hair. Maybe, Lucy thought, one of my sons is too well dressed. She slammed the door and turned the key in the ignition. The Land Rover started with an awesome roar.

She glanced at Sam as she put the Rover in gear.

"Those kids look like me twenty years ago."

Sam looked at her noncommittally.

"When you ran away from home, hitchhiked to Berkeley, spent the night in Golden Gate Park, and begged for spare change in the morning?"

"Oh," Lucy replied. "So you've heard this story before?"

Sam nodded sagely. "So many times, I'm starting to think it happened to *me*."

Maybe, Lucy thought, it was time she just shut up and drove. They'd get to her father's house in a moment. Then they could all settle back and relax.

And after that they could worry about just what they were going to do with the rest of their lives.

Three

They were here at last. At least he thought this had to be his grandfather's house.

Michael couldn't remember the last time they had been here. He guessed he'd been pretty young at the time. His father and grandfather hadn't exactly gotten along. In fact, the last time the two of them had seen each other had been Grandmother's funeral. Michael didn't remember that very well, either, but he did remember his mother's story about how the two men had almost gotten into a fistfight at Grandmother's graveside.

There had been the occasional phone call and a few brief visits in the last couple of years, but neither Michael nor Sam really knew their grandfather very well. Still, from what he had heard about the old man, this place they were driving toward suited him.

First off, the place was out of the way. Michael had followed his mother's Land Rover on his motorbike, all the way through town along the beach highway. They had turned off at last on this long, winding road bordered on either side by pine trees. It was so different from the town; just a turn in the road and they went from bright, noisy action to cool, quiet shade. It was all a little weird, really. It was hard for Michael to believe that there could be a place like this in Santa Carla.

They had pulled into the driveway of a house that certainly fit the neighborhood. Actually Grandpa's place wasn't exactly a house, at least, not like they had houses back in Phoenix. Oh, it was plenty big enough. It just looked a little rough around the edges, like somebody had crossed a log cabin with one of those big, sprawling places you always saw in horror movies. Michael wondered if it looked that strange inside.

There was somebody lying on the front porch, actually lying there, right on the floor. Michael pulled his bike up next to the Land Rover. He flipped down the kickstand and went to stand next to his mother and brother, who were staring up at the man on the porch. The man hadn't moved since they'd arrived.

"Grandpa?" Sam asked in a hushed voice.

Their mother nodded, and whispered, "Must be asleep."

The three of them approached Grandpa as quietly as they could.

He wasn't dressed the way Michael remembered him, dark suit, tie, sort of like his father, only older. Now Grandpa wore jeans and a work shirt. He had Indian moccasins on his feet, the kind with all the multicolored beads, and what white hair he had left was tied behind his head in a braid.

Michael led the way up the stairs. Grandpa still didn't move. Michael stopped, just short of where the old man lay.

"He looks dead," Michael said after a moment's pause.

His mother dismissed his observation with a wave of her hands. "He's just a deep sleeper."

Michael pointed at Grandpa's face. "He's not breathing, Mom."

Mother frowned and stepped forward, placing her palm on the still man's forehead. Sam walked up beside her.

"If he's dead," Sam asked, "can we move back to Phoenix?"

Then Grandpa opened his eyes. Michael took a step back. He heard his mother make a little noise in her throat.

Grandpa smiled.

"Playin' dead," he remarked. "And from what I heard, doin' a damn good job of it too."

The old man sat up, and their mother leaned forward to hug him. Michael turned to look at Sam. From his brother's expression he could tell Sam felt pretty much the same way about what was going on.

Weird. And it was getting weirder every minute.

Their mother smiled back at the two of them.

"Well," she said brightly, "why don't you boys go unload the truck and we'll get settled in?"

Settled in? Michael glanced at his brother a final time. Well, there was no helping it. The two condemned boys walked down the stairs to obey their mother's orders. Michael grabbed his barbells from the back corner of the trailer and carried them glumly through the front door.

Once he walked inside the house, he decided he might want to change his mind. The place sprawled out every which way. It would probably take them half an hour to explore it. But the living room was great, filled with old, comfortable, leather-covered couches, with Indian blankets on the floor and all sorts of wild pictures on the wall. There was a huge fireplace in the middle of the room and two staircases on either side that led to a balcony above. Plus, just in front of the fireplace, staring right at Michael, was a stuffed mountain lion.

Sam struggled past him, his arms laden with one of the incredibly heavy boxes that contained a mere portion of his massive comic book collection.

"This is kind of a cool place," Michael remarked.

Sam grunted as he placed his burden on the floor. He stared at the mountain lion.

"Yeah," he agreed. "For the *Texas Chainsaw Massacre*."

Michael gave his brother what he hoped was a withering look. "Come on. Will you give Mom a break?"

It was time to get rid of his own burden. Michael

hefted the barbells he was carrying and headed through the kitchen toward the porch. Sam followed right behind him.

Michael pushed open the back door with his weights. Sam brought up the rear, letting the screen door slam after him. Michael looked out at the backyard as he pumped the weights a couple of times. You couldn't see anybody else's house out here. It was like they were all alone, miles and miles away from civilization.

Sam pointed back at the house.

"What's wrong with this picture?" he asked.

Michael shrugged, then pumped again.

"No TV," his brother informed him. "Have you seen a TV?" Sam frowned. "No TV means no MTV."

Michael put down the weights at last and looked straight at his brother.

"Hey, Sam, we are flat broke."

His brother's eyes widened, as if only now did he realize the true horror of his situation.

"Even poor people have TVs," he said at last.

Nanook couldn't stop barking. He was probably the happiest dog in the universe, Lucy thought. There was a field full of horses just behind her father's yard. Nanook had decided he liked the horses and was more than happy to tell the world about it.

Her father had crawled into the U-Haul and was passing boxes and odds and ends out to Lucy. She marveled at how spry he had managed to stay. But then, she marveled at a lot of things about her father. Understanding had never been a strong suit between them. She wasn't even sure they still knew how to talk to each other. Heaven knew they hadn't done much talking so far. Still, Lucy knew that sooner or later her father would get around to saying what was on his mind.

He grunted as he handed her a framed picture. From the look on his face Lucy could tell he didn't much approve of the modernistic subject matter; cubes within cubes within cubes. She laid it down on the ground so that the boys could carry it up to the house. When she looked back at the trailer, she saw her father regarding her with a contemplative look she knew all too well. He had had enough of unpacking for the moment. He was about to grace her with his opinion.

"Lucy," he said as he dismounted the trailer to stand next to her, "you're the only woman I ever knew who didn't improve her situation by getting divorced."

So here it was. The Divorce Discussion. Well, she had rehearsed this one in her head a long time before she'd gotten here.

"Oh, Dad. A big legal war wasn't going to improve anybody's situation. We've all been through enough." That was the rehearsed part. On impulse she hugged him.

"Besides," she added, "I was raised better than that."

"Ouch!" he yelled. "My hair!"

Lucy laughed when she realized her hug had caught his braid. She gently freed the long strand of hair from her grip.

"Look at you," she said with a smile. "When I dressed like that, you threw me out of the house." She sighed. "I used to hate your short hair and your uptight suits. Then I went ahead and married one." She shook her head. "Now look at you. We're still out of synch."

Her father laughed. "Well, maybe we can work on it a little." He grabbed the framed picture and started to carry it to the house.

Lucy watched him as he disappeared through the front door. Maybe this time they could really work on it, after all.

This looked like the best room in the place. Michael steered the sheets and blankets he held through the narrow doorway.

Sam was already in there, stacking comic books on the shelves.

"What have you got there?" his brother demanded. "Flannel sheets? Oh, boy!" He rolled his eyes up toward the ceiling. "I knew *something* around here would cheer me up!"

Michael decided to ignore his brother's sarcasm. He laid the bedclothes on the bed. This place was big, and close to the stairs and the bathroom, and it had a great view of the backyard. He liked this room even more now, much too much to give it up. There was only one way to handle this situation.

"This room is mine," he said simply.

Sam turned around and spread out his arms, as if to protect his comic collection.

"I was here first!"

Michael nodded. There was also only one way to handle younger brothers.

"Okay," he said calmly. "I'll flip you for it."

Sam glared back at Michael, but he didn't speak. He knew as well as Michael that older brothers usually win out in the end. But Sam also knew that Michael's offer was his only chance.

"Okay," Sam said slowly, as if he had to drag the two syllables from his lungs.

Michael laughed, grabbed Sam, and flipped him upside down. This will show the little bugger! Thinking of Sam as a bugger made him laugh even harder.

Michael gasped as white-hot pain shot through his body. He looked down to see Sam biting his thigh.

"Owww!" Michael pushed Sam away with what energy he had left. "You little shit!"

Sam was up and running as soon as his brother had let him go. Michael stood up, wincing at the pain. The little bugger wasn't going to get away with this! Michael ran out the door and down the stairs in hot pursuit.

"Help me, Mom!" Sam screamed. "Help!"

They were running down the back staircase. Their mother was walking up the staircase in front, a box in her hands. She nodded pleasantly to Sam.

"Soon," was all she said.

Sam ran into the living room. Michael couldn't help but smile. There was no way his brother could get by him now. Justice would be served at last.

Sam turned and started clawing at what Michael had first thought was a wall. But no, when he looked at their outline beneath the ceiling, Michael realized they were large sliding doors! With a gasp of triumph Sam tore one of them open and ran into the next room. Michael ran close behind him.

He took one step into the room and stopped dead.

Four

A thousand eyes stared down at them.

Both Michael and Sam looked cautiously around the room, their fight forgotten.

An owl glared at them from above the double doors. Next to it was a squirrel and a raccoon. On the shelf next to the door stood a cardinal, a crow, and a big gray tomcat.

It took Michael a minute to realize that this crowd of unmoving, staring beasts wasn't alive. They weren't moving because all of them were stuffed. Michael reached out and stroked the back of a nearby skunk. On other shelves were piles of pelts and wooden forms in the shapes of various animals. And there were boxes, lots and lots of boxes.

Sam pulled down a shoe box from a nearby shelf. It was full of eyes, glass eyes, some very small, others larger than those in Sam's head. Sam hastily returned the box to its resting place.

"Rules!"

The shout came from behind them. Sam and Michael jumped as one. They turned around as quickly as they could. Grandpa stood behind them.

"Got some rules around here," Grandpa remarked. He waved for the two of them to follow him. Sam and Michael glanced at each other, then trailed after their grandfather into the kitchen.

Grandpa opened the door to the refrigerator. Inside,

hanging from the middle shelf, was a hand-lettered cardboard sign bearing the words OLD FART.

"Second shelf is mine." Grandpa pointed at the sign for emphasis. "Keep my root beer and double-thick Mint Oreo cookies here. Nobody touches the second shelf."

Grandpa closed the door and waved for the two of them to follow again. Michael glanced out the window as he turned to continue the guided tour. He recognized a small green bush growing by the corner of the house. A small green marijuana bush. This, he thought, could explain a lot. He nudged his brother and pointed to his discovery.

Sam shook his head and looked back at Michael, puzzled.

Younger brothers! Didn't they know anything? Michael pressed his forefinger and thumb together, then put them to his lips, inhaling deeply.

Grandpa had already disappeared into the living room. They had to hurry to keep up. On the far side of the room their mother was carting one last load of clothes upstairs.

Michael caught up with his grandfather first. The old man had been silent since he had issued his instructions at the refrigerator. He seemed to be better at leading around than at talking. Michael realized that Grandpa might be as uncertain of how to react to them as they were around him. He supposed it made sense. Their father and grandfather had never gotten along, so Grandpa had always stayed away. They had hardly seen each other in years.

Michael cleared his throat. He wasn't going to be able to stay in a house with a guy who never talked. Maybe he should be the one to start the conversation going. Besides, there were things about this town he had to find out.

He told his grandfather about the spray-painted sign he had seen on the back of WELCOME TO SANTA CARLA.

Grandpa grunted in response.

Well, that didn't start anything. Michael decided to try a more direct approach.

"Is Santa Carla really the murder capital?"

Grandpa paused and nodded. "Got some bad elements around here."

"Wait a minute." Sam tugged at Michael's sleeve. "Wait. I want to get one thing straight. We have moved to the murder capital of the world?"

He pushed past Michael to get to the source.

"Are you serious, Grandpa?"

Their grandfather scratched absently at his mustache. "Well, let me put it this way: If all the corpses buried around here were to stand up, we'd have a population problem."

Sam and Michael looked at each other again. The situation in Santa Carla was not improving.

"Now," their grandfather continued, "when the mailman brings the *TV Guide* on Wednesdays, sometimes the corner of the address label will curl up. You'll be tempted to peel it off. Don't. You'll end up ripping the cover, and I don't like that."

He walked into the stuffed-animal room and turned to face them.

"And stay outa here."

"You have a TV?" Sam asked, hope springing anew.

"No." Grandpa shook his head. "I just like to read *TV Guide*. Read the *TV Guide*, you don't need a TV."

And with that he shut the door.

They had managed to all sit down and eat dinner without having a fight. That was a positive sign. And Sam had given up the room with only a couple minutes of shouting. Michael had to admit that they were settling in here fairly well.

Sam was in the living room, trying to set up the stereo. Every once in a while a note or two would blast into the kitchen before Sam lost it again. Nanook wandered into the living room to bark encouragement.

His mother handed Michael a just washed platter for him to dry. They were alone in the kitchen, just quietly doing the dishes. He rubbed hard at the large plate, his dish towel squeaking along the rim. Maybe it would work here, after all. He'd thought about this all afternoon as he got his room in order. Maybe this was the place he'd really get control of what he wanted to do, who he wanted to be. Maybe Santa Carla would be the fresh start their mother had been talking about, after all.

He'd made another decision this afternoon too. He put the platter down at the back of the dish rack. There'd be no better time to tell her than now.

"Mom," Michael began. "I think I'd like to get a job."

His mother looked up from the sink, a question in her eyes. She didn't ask it.

"School's only a few weeks away," she mentioned.

He took another plate from her hands. He dried it for a moment before he spoke again. "I was thinking of not going back to school."

The stereo kicked to life in the other room. His mother frowned at Michael. He didn't want to hear what she had to say. What was the song playing in the other room? It was another oldie.

Sam rushed into the room with Nanook close behind.

"Come on, Mom!" he yelled. "The sixties live again! It's Pony time!" He grabbed their mother's hand and pulled her away from the sink.

Michael remembered to breathe again. Saved by the song. What was that music? "Land of a Thousand Dances"? Something like that. He couldn't remember. It was whatever song had that Na-nananana stuff in it. The lyrics didn't make much sense. What exactly was the Mashed Potato, anyway?

Mom and Sam boogied all over the kitchen, while Nanook

barked for emphasis. The two of them danced in his direction, reaching out to drag him in.

Michael shook his head and backed away. He didn't know exactly what he wanted to do. But he really didn't feel much like dancing.

Five

The night was alive. Michael had never seen anything like it. The beach was full of people. There were bonfires everywhere, almost to the edge of the boardwalk. And every bonfire seemed to have attracted a hundred kids who bounced around the flames like moths.

Michael walked around the edge of the crowd. He and Sam had escaped from the house just after "Night of a Thousand Dances," before his mother could ask any more questions. How could he explain to her how important it was for him to change his life? If that meant leaving school behind and getting a job, he was ready to do it. But he knew that kind of thinking didn't fit in with his mother's "values," the sort of things she always said she "expected from her sons." He didn't think she'd ever understand.

Rock music blasted all around them. A band played up ahead on a makeshift stage, their songs mixing with noise from a dozen boom boxes around the bonfires. Michael's feet hit the sand in time with the beat. He was glad he didn't have to do any explaining yet. It was good just to be outside. It was time he and Sam found out about Santa Carla for themselves.

A young blond girl almost ran into them. She laughed and waved as she ran away, leaping over a prone couple who seemed to be very involved with each other. Whether or not it was the "murder capital," it sure was a lot wilder than Phoenix. And Michael decided he liked it. He wanted to look everywhere, to see and hear everything.

Michael shook his head as the crowd shouted with a song, a noise so loud that it almost set his ears ringing. There were so many people. He was sure some of them were runaways and drifters, just looking for a good time. A few of those might be trouble, he imagined. With a crowd like this there were bound to be some drug dealers too. He wondered if that mix of drifters and drugs could make this the "murder capital."

He probably would never know. Michael decided it wasn't worth worrying about. He doubted anything really violent could happen out on the beach. There were too many people, all of them moving, jumping, dancing to the constant beat. It was almost like a tribal thing, a huge crowd all together as one. Maybe, Michael thought, that's why this place attracted so many ex-hippies. Maybe that was even why his Woodstock-era mother had brought them here.

Michael had to stop to let his brother catch up. Sam scuffed his new shoes in the sand. He didn't seem to be having a good time at all. It had taken him five minutes before he left the house to make sure his hair was just right, that his clothes were just the right combination of Matthew Broderick and Judd Nelson. Now, Michael was sure, he was all too aware of all the other teenagers jumping and shouting. It was a wild crowd, dressed for summer and the beach, wearing everything from skimpy bathing suits to sweatshirts and jeans. There was only one way they weren't dressed: There didn't seem to be a brat-packer among them. Sam looked like he came from another world.

Sam stared down at the sand. "Wanna change my clothes, my hair, my face," he muttered.

Michael laughed. His brother had been traumatized by too much life in junior high. "Will you stop worrying about your clothes?"

Sam pulled absently at the pleat of his trousers. "Just because you buy yours by the pound."

Michael tugged on his brother's arm and led him up a set of stairs close to the stage. He was going to get to the center of the action, and he wasn't going to let his little brother's moping slow him down. The music was even louder here. It seemed to surround them. Michael could feel the drums pound through the sandy stairs. The wailing guitars pressed against his bare face and arms. He shut his eyes and could feel the singer's words behind his eyelids. He swayed back and forth, carried away as the music flowed through his muscles; the beat pumped blood through his veins.

He opened his eyes and looked out over the crowd. Everybody was moving, laughing, having fun. Yeah, Michael thought. What could be better than this?

That was when he saw her.

Her long, dark hair cascaded in ringlets around her beautiful face and brushed softly against her bare shoulders. She was dressed all in lace, like a gypsy, or a girl from a fairy tale. Her clothes might look ordinary on some other girl. On her, well—Michael had to remember to breathe.

He had never seen anyone like her before. There had been girls in Phoenix, but they had just been girls. How could he describe it? Everything about her was just right.

She was in the middle of the crowd, but Michael couldn't see anyone but her. It was as if they were the only two people truly alive, really listening to the music, as if the thousand others around them had just been put here for show. When she danced, she was dancing just for him. When she smiled that sweet, sad smile, Michael knew just what she felt.

Sam said something behind him. He couldn't really hear the words. He couldn't take his eyes off her. There was a tightness in his chest as he watched her, but it was a wonderful tightness.

And then she looked at him, straight into his eyes. Michael knew, in that instant, he had not been fooling himself. She saw something in him, too, something that she needed. It was plain in her eyes, the way her forehead creased, the way her mouth opened just so.

Michael smiled at her. She looked away for a second, then met his gaze again. Michael felt she wanted to smile too. Why didn't she?

She looked away again and grabbed the hand of a sandy-haired boy who was even younger than Sam by a couple years. Michael guessed he might be ten or eleven. He had the same sad face as the girl, probably brother and sister. She turned and pulled the youngster into the crowd.

"Sam!" Michael yelled.

"Huh?" His brother looked away from the rock band. Michael grabbed hold of Sam's arm and started to run for the spot where the girl disappeared. He ignored his brother's protests, content for the moment to drag him along. After all, how could Michael explain, especially to a younger brother, that he had just found his reason for living?

Six

It certainly was festive here. Bright lights, restaurants, and stores open until all hours of the night. It was quite a change from Phoenix.

Lucy hoped that it was the right kind of change. Not just for her but for the boys. They had been through so much with the divorce. Both of them were smart; she knew that. And both of them were pretty sensible, too, most of the time. But she was pretty sure that Michael, especially, still had some emotions locked up inside of him that he just wasn't letting out. She just hoped he could find some way to express those feelings without hurting himself.

Well, he was almost grown now. She really couldn't keep him too close to the nest anymore. He had to try things on his own. That's why she had let the two boys go down to the Boardwalk so soon, to get a sense of their new home and maybe unwind some of those tensions they still held inside. Besides which, she made the two of them promise to stay together. It was safer that way. She figured, even at the worst of times, they had enough common sense to keep at least one brain working between the two of them.

But that big old house of her father's had seemed awfully quiet once the boys had left. Grandpa had retreated to the taxidermy room to stuff his animals. There was no TV; she really didn't feel like reading. Besides, it was a nice summer night, perfect for a walk.

She decided it was time to get reacquainted with Santa Carla. She changed into a soft blue summer blouse and khaki skirt and went for a stroll on the pier.

The sound of rock and roll power chords drifted from the distant beach. There was a rock band playing out there tonight on the edge of the Boardwalk, with maybe a thousand kids watching them, including, she imagined, her sons. That was nice. Sam and Michael should really enjoy themselves.

She was just as glad she wasn't there herself. Once, she had loved being the center of all that noise and action. Now it just made her ears hurt. She laughed softly to herself. Aversion to rock bands. One of the first signs of old age.

These days, the so-called "pier" was more her speed. It was actually a street of shops and restaurants, built on a wide, wooden platform over the water. She was surprised at the diversity of the places out here now. When she was a girl, there had been nothing but bars and places to buy things that bore the legend "Souvenir of Santa Carla" but were actually made in Hong Kong. Since then (and Lucy realized it had probably been twenty years), the pier had gone upscale. Oh, some of the places along here now were still tourist traps, but some of them were quite nice; a bit overpriced, perhaps, because of their location, but many were actually filled with interesting crafts and useful clothing.

She'd have to come back here when she had more money.

If she ever had more money. Lucy sighed. It was her first night back in Santa Carla. She needed time to settle in. She really shouldn't have to worry about jobs, money, and real life. Not yet. Leave it for tomorrow and the daylight.

A small crowd had gathered nearby, listening to a speaker

of some sort. She wandered over toward the entertainment, hoping it would take her mind off other things.

"You will be saved!"

She stopped at the edge of the crowd. A scrawny man called to the crowd from the front steps of a store that had closed for the night. He was dressed in bell-bottoms and a faded, flowered shirt, as if, Lucy thought, he hadn't changed his clothes in twenty years. His long, lank hair fell in his face as he shouted.

"All of you! Saved"—he lurched across the steps, his right hand waving aloft—"from the sin of Santa Carla! Saved! All of you! All of you!"

The old hippie paused, uncertain, as if he had memorized his speech and had temporarily lost his place. Lucy still watched him, but her mind was elsewhere.

We all used to look like that once, she thought. How out of place this unwashed, half-crazed man looked now. How much we've all changed. For better or worse, most of us had moved on from the late sixties, left the drugs and free love and protest marches behind. And life wasn't any the worse for it, really. It was just different.

The old hippie walked back and forth across the step, mumbling softly to himself, as if moving might jar his memory. Lucy had seen far too many people like him before. Maybe he had taken a few too many acid trips. Or maybe he was one of those who couldn't accept that the world had changed, whose mind could only hold on to one sliver of time when things seemed right. Whatever had done it, most of his brain seemed to be gone. What little was left seemed to have turned to religion, at least after a fashion.

"Confront your sins!" The hippie smiled at the crowd. "That's what it is! What you have to do!" He turned and pointed, straight toward Lucy. "Santa Carla, you can still be saved!"

The couple standing next to her looked her way. Lucy shrugged. "I think I used to date that guy."

The couple laughed and walked away. Lucy turned to continue her exploration of the pier. She stopped at a kiosk covered with notes and flyers. Apartments for rent, boats for hire, self-realization seminars, missing children, but no notes saying "Help Wanted." Just how hard was it going to be to find a job around here?

"Excuse me," a woman's voice called softly past Lucy's shoulder. Lucy stepped out of the way and watched a thin woman tape a new flyer over the others. There was a picture of a large man and the words:

MISSING

Security Guard Edward Winowski, also known as "Big Ed"

Lucy didn't read any further. The thin woman had two small children with her. She guessed that the man in the picture must be their father. What could have happened to him? Could he have run away from his family?

The thin woman looked up at Lucy as she walked past. Her eyes were so sad. Maybe, Lucy thought, there were worse things than getting divorced and moving away from everything you've known for the last seventeen years. She hoped the woman and her children would be all right.

Lucy stopped in front of a restaurant. There was a help-wanted sign in the window. Maybe there was a job here, after all. Still, she'd have to be cautious. She walked over to take a closer look. From what she had heard about the employment situation around here, a place might have to have real problems to have any kind of a job opening at all.

There was a child crying near the sign. It was a young boy, maybe three or four. He looked very lost.

Lucy squatted down beside him. She asked the boy what his name was. He just kept on crying. She asked him if his parents were around. No response, only tears.

Lucy looked around. She'd bet the parents were somewhere nearby. There was a well-lit store right next to the restaurant, a place with a bright neon sign that read MAX'S VIDEO. Maybe the boy had just wandered out of there.

She scooped the child up in her arms. Four teenagers entered the shop in front of her. They were dressed in kind of an odd style. One of them wore an old tux, another embroidered denim. Each one of their jackets was different from anything she'd seen teenagers around here wearing. Probably some sort of teenage fashion statement. She had other things to worry about right now.

"C'mon," she said to her small charge. "You're not going to be lost anymore." She followed the youths into the video store.

The door buzzed as she opened it.

A tall man with curly, dark hair and glasses turned from where he had been watching the teens. His frown turned into a smile as he saw Lucy walk in the store. It was quite a nice smile, open and friendly. There was a dog with him behind the counter, a dog that continued to growl at the youths browsing the racks. An attractive young black woman by the cash register pointedly ignored the four boys as they walked back and forth in front of her.

Oh dear, Lucy thought. Looks like I've walked into the middle of a local crisis. Well, that couldn't be helped. She had an upset child that needed to be taken care of. She walked up to the man at the counter.

"This boy seems to be lost," she began. She glanced around the store. Besides the youths, there were four other customers. "I thought maybe his parents might be in here?"

"Well, let's see," the man behind the counter replied as he also looked around the store. He had a nice voice, Lucy thought, warm and deep, the kind of voice you immediately trusted.

The door buzzed again. A woman in her early twenties rushed in and across the store.

"Terry!" she called to the child. "Oh, thank God! I was so worried!"

Terry held out his arms to his mother. Lucy dutifully handed the boy, now no longer crying, to the other woman.

"I don't know how to thank you," the woman began. Lucy replied that no thanks were necessary. The man behind the counter reached into a jar and handed Terry a lollipop. The mother backed out of the store, thanking them both again.

"How about you?" the man asked Lucy. She looked at him and realized he was holding another lollipop out for her.

"No thanks." She smiled and shook her head.

The teenagers walked past them. The man's smile was gone. He spoke to the blond boy in the lead.

"I told you not to come in here anymore."

The blond boy only smiled. He led his followers from the store.

The man behind the counter nodded after them as they left. "Wild kids."

Lucy looked out the window as the four boys climbed on their motorcycles and revved their engines. They peeled out one by one, off the pier and onto the beach road.

"Oh," she said to the counterman, "they're just young. We were that age, too, once. Only *they* dress better than we ever did."

"A generous nature," the man replied with a laugh. "I like that in a person. My name is Max." He pointed to his dog, much quieter now that the teenagers were gone. "This is Thorn."

"Lucy," she replied with a smile.

Max grinned back. "So what can I help you find tonight, Lucy? We've got it all. The best selection in Santa Carla."

Lucy glanced around at the store, really taking it all in for the first time. There were a dozen TV screens behind Max, all showing different programs: rock singers in tight pants, Bugs Bunny outwitting Yosemite Sam, John Wayne with six-gun in hand, an old black-and-white film with an overweight corpse rising from a grave. Rock music blared from speakers overhead; as far as Lucy could figure out, it didn't go with any of the programs on the screens. It was all a bit overwhelming.

She looked back at Max. He was still smiling. Should she tell him? She paused a second, then decided, Why not? She doubted she'd find anybody friendlier around here.

"I'm not looking for a tape," she began. "What I really need is—"

"A job." Max finished the sentence for her.

"Do I look that needy?" Lucy felt her cheeks flush.

Max shook his head and laughed. "I just have ways of knowing these things. It comes from living in a resort town for too long." He walked down to the end of the counter and pulled out a couple of straight-backed chairs. "Why don't we talk about it?"

Lucy decided there could be worse things to do on a summer evening than talking with a handsome man about the possibilities of employment. And there was also something about him—it showed in the way he moved and talked—something that said he had been through it all, just like Lucy, and had somehow come **through** it to find himself, happy and alive, on the other side.

Whoa, Lucy! she told herself. There she went again, elaborating on first impressions, for God's sake. But Max seemed so different from her nervous, success-starved husband.

Ex-husband, she reminded herself. It certainly wouldn't hurt to talk.

Max waved her to a chair. She nodded pleasantly to him and sat.

Things seemed to happen fast in Santa Carla.

Seven

Sam had had just about enough of older brothers. First Michael had gotten the room that Sam had had first dibs on. But that wasn't bad enough. Oh, no. Now his older brother was going to drag him all over Santa Carla and never tell him why.

Sam caught up with his brother, who had just run them both halfway down the length of the Boardwalk. "Where are we going?"

"Nowhere." Michael didn't even look at him.

"Then what's our rush?" Sam tried to run a step ahead so his brother would have to acknowledge his existence. "You're chasing after that girl! Why don't you admit it? I'm at the mercy of your sex glands!"

Michael stopped dead. He looked at his brother at last, and the look wasn't particularly friendly.

"Don't you have something better to do with your time than follow me around all night?"

He wondered if he should remind Michael that they promised their mother they would stay together. Sam was sure his mother forced this promise out of them more for his benefit than his brother's. But it was getting pretty obvious that right now Michael didn't want a younger brother around.

So whose orders was he going to follow, Michael's or their mother's? Sam glanced at the storefronts behind them, killing time until he could figure out what to do.

Behind him was a store window full of comic books.

Even better, the sign on the window read FROG'S COMICS. That meant the whole store was full of them.

Maybe, Sam thought, there was something worthwhile in Santa Carla, after all.

He turned back to his brother. Heck, Michael could take care of himself. So could Sam, with a comic-book store around.

"As a matter of fact, I do have something better," Sam replied. Michael nodded absently, obviously glad to be free of his burden, and hurried on down the Boardwalk.

Sam turned and entered the promised land.

The first thing that hit him were the colors. There were comic books everywhere. They hung from the ceiling, they were tacked to the walls, they were crammed into a dozen long bins. What light there was—Sam could see a few dim bulbs overhead—shone off the plastic bags that held a thousand different comic treasures. Their garish covers beckoned him inside; the overmuscled men in red and blue held Sam in a trance as he walked down the center aisle.

The second thing that hit him was the smell, a certain musty odor that only came from huge quantities of decaying paper—the cheap paper that comics were always printed on—mixed in with dust and human sweat. Sam breathed deeply. This was the stuff of life. This dim, crowded, and grimy place was a *real* comic-book store.

The third thing he noticed was that he was being watched. He got that creepy feeling on the back of his neck, like a pair of eyes were staring at his spine. A kid, close to his age, dressed like he had stepped out of a Rambo film, had glowered at him as he passed. Sam thought it might be better not to turn around and look at him again.

But what was he worried about? He wasn't doing anything wrong. No one had even talked to him, much less done anything threatening. It was just nerves, he told himself. Just going into a new place. Come to think of it, this dark little store was a little creepy. Every corner of every surface was covered; comics and magazines hung down from the rafters. There was no empty space anywhere, just all these comics closing in on every side.

Nerves, Sam told himself again. He decided to look through one of the racks that lined the far wall. Maybe it would be a little more open over there.

He passed another kid in khaki fatigues. This time, he was sure the guy's eyes were following him.

What was going on here? He turned down another aisle and headed slowly past more rows of comics, casually heading toward the door. Ahead of him he could see a counter with an ancient cash register. A couple, close to his mother's age, leaned against the back wall. Their resemblance to his mother ended with age. Besides that, they looked like they had stepped off the cover of an old Mamas and Papas album, long hair, faded clothes and all. Since Sam and his family had gotten into town this afternoon he had seen maybe a dozen other people who looked the same way. There seemed to be a lot of old hippies in Santa Carla.

The older people didn't pay any attention to Sam at all. They stared, hypnotized by the program on a small TV. Sam glanced at the screen. A woman had just screamed. Christopher Lee was getting impaled by a bush. Sam nodded his head sagely. That meant it was *Scars of Dracula*.

When he looked back to the aisle, he saw one of the khaki pair quickly moving toward him. He heard footsteps behind him too. The two of them were closing in.

"Ah—" Sam swallowed. "Got a problem, guys?"

The two of them stopped close by his sides. Sam leaned against the bin behind him and tried to smile casually.

The one who had come from the direction of the counter nodded at him. "Just scoping your civilian wardrobe."

"Oh." Sam glanced at his clothes. "Pretty cool, huh?"

"Yeah," the other half of the pair replied, "'for a 'fashion victim.' ''

"If you're looking for the diet frozen yogurt bar," the first one added, "it went out of business last summer."

So this was it. His first real challenge in Santa Carla. Sam had to cool these guys out fast.

"Actually," he admitted, the slightest touch of boredom in his voice, "I was looking for a particular *Batman*. Series E, Volume 26, Issue 14?"

The two commandos looked at each other.

"That's a very serious book, man," the first one said.

"Very serious," the other agreed. "Only five in existence."

"Four, actually," Sam replied with the slightest hint of a smile. "And I'm always on the lookout for the other three."

The fatigue twins both stared at him, their mouths opened in awe. Sam had them now! He had to be careful not to break into a big grin. If he played this right, he could become a legend around here before the summer was through.

"Now, you look at these bins!" Sam turned around and flipped rapidly through the comics. "You can't put a *Superman* #77 in with the #200s!" He looked up at the two others, who hovered just past his shoulders. He waved the #77 in the first one's face. "They haven't even discovered Red Kryptonite yet!" He went back to the bins. "Or this #98 in with the #300s. I mean, Lori Lemaris the Mermaid hasn't even been introduced!"

The first commando leaned even farther forward. "Where the hell are you from, Krypton?"

"Phoenix, actually," Sam replied. "But, lucky me, we've moved to this cultural metropolis. And since there is obviously nothing to do here except work on my superior comic-book collection, you'll probably be seeing a lot of me. Lucky you."

The two soldiers stepped back to look at each other. Sam took a moment to get his first really good look at the two of them. They looked like brothers, both with short dark hair cropped so close to their heads that it barely showed beyond their green berets. Their bodies were compact and muscular, as if they had both gone through a lot of basic training. Sam decided that if he had a choice, he'd just as soon have the pair of them on his side.

The two nodded once at each other, a single shake of the head with no wasted motion. The first one turned his emotionless face to regard Sam.

"Okay," he said. "I'm Edgar." He pointed to the other boy. "This is Alan. We're the Frog Brothers."

Sam smiled and introduced himself. The Frog Brothers stared at him impassively.

"Here," Edgar said after a moment. "Take this." He held a comic in his hand.

What was this, a token of friendship? Sam accepted the Frogs' offering. The two continued to stare at him.

"Is it free?" Sam asked.

"Free?" Edgar replied. He shook his head. "This is Santa Carla, not Santa Claus."

Alan stuck his palm in front of Sam's nose.

"Buck and a quarter," he added.

Sam looked at the comic in his hand. It was one of those horror books from the early fifties, before they had a comics code. It wasn't an EC or some other major book, either; Sam had never even heard of the title, lurid red letters on a gray background: *Vampires Everywhere*.

Sam shook his head. "I don't like horror comics." He held the comic book out to give it back to the Frogs.

Edgar didn't make any move to take the comic back. "You'll like this one, Sam from Phoenix."

He paused as the front door opened. An older teenager with a shaved head walked inside.

Edgar looked straight into Sam's eyes.

"This comic could save your life."

Shaved Head reached quickly across one of the bins and ripped a pair of comics from the wall, thumbtacks and all.

"Hey!" Edgar and Alan yelled as one. "Surf Nazis!"

Shaved Head laughed and ran from the shop. The Frog Brothers took off after him.

The older man behind the counter, who Sam guessed was Mr. Frog, looked up from his TV. He blinked, confused, as if what had just happened in the store was an outtake from some movie he had just wandered into. He raised a finger indecisively, then, after a moment, pointed it in the general direction of the door.

"Hey," he repeated, then turned back to his real movie.

Sam decided he had had enough of this place for now. He quickly bought the comic book and left. There were some things he had to think about. Why had the Frogs given him this particular comic? And what about that guy who had swiped the books? Edgar and Alan had called him a Surf Nazi. Surf Nazis? What kind of a town was this, anyway?

Eight

"Hey!" Michael yelled as the overmuscled jerk in the Surf Nazis jacket shoved his way past him. The jerk paid no attention but ran on ahead, quickly passing the pair Michael was following.

Michael had found the girl and younger boy right after he had gotten rid of Sam. He had turned the corner just beyond the comic shop, and there they were, less than a block away.

Two thoughts jumped into Michael's head the moment he saw her. One was that she looked even more beautiful than when he had first seen her in the crowd. Her bare shoulders and white vest were bright under the streetlights. She glided along the street with the kid by her side, pausing to look in a store window here, talking and laughing with the boy a second later, her every movement silhouetted against the night.

Michael's second thought was that he didn't have the slightest idea what he could say to her. He had been so afraid that he might lose her that he had run after her the minute she had left the crowd. He had searched the Boardwalk in a panic, afraid that if he didn't find her at once, she would be gone forever.

Now, suddenly, here she was.

Michael didn't know what to do next. He started to follow them, walking slowly, glancing in store windows himself, as if he were doing nothing but taking an evening walk. He didn't want to get too close to them just yet, not until he had come up with something to say. But he didn't want to lose her again, either. So he walked, hoping for that something, the right thing, a word, a sentence, a smile that would make her laugh the way she had back in front of the rock band, something that would make her see him the way he looked at her. Something just had to come to him!

Two others ran past him, younger than the Surf Nazi, both dressed in what looked like some sort of army-surplus camouflage gear. Michael looked ahead and stopped walking.

She was looking back at him over her shoulder. She paused as the two kids ran past her, then turned to face Michael.

"Are you following me?" she asked. Her voice was clear and high and beautiful.

"Well, I—" Michael began. What could he say?

She took a step toward him. "Did you want to talk to me?"

"Well—" Michael could feel his cheeks flushing. Don't be an idiot! he told himself. He had to say something! "Yeah. Sure."

"Okay," she replied. "Talk."

"I just wanted to . . ." His voice died as if he had no more breath in his lungs. He cleared his throat and tried again. "I, uh—"

"Hey, Michael!" Feet ran up the street behind him. It was Sam. "Mom's here!"

His brother clattered to a halt a few feet in front of Michael. Sam was waving a comic book around in his hand. Michael looked over his brother's head at the girl.

She laughed and grabbed the hand of the young boy. "Nice talking to you!"

"Wait!" Michael called, but they were already out of sight around a corner.

He wasn't going to lose her now! He dodged by Sam at a run.

He stopped when he reached the corner.

The girl and the small fry had turned to look at him. And they were surrounded by others, all of them on motorcycles, real machines, the kind Michael dreamed about. All he had, really, was a glorified motorbike. These were real choppers, stripped down, customized jobs that could really move.

There were four bikes, and each one had a rider, guys close to Michael's age, at most a year or two older. Three of them wore dark coats; the blond guy's coat was so big, it sort of looked like a cloak. The other one's jacket was embroidered denim. Their hair was longer than Michael was used to seeing, but they weren't scruffy like the middle-aged hippies or weird like the Surf Nazis. They all looked like they knew what they wanted. They looked more together than any teenagers Michael had ever seen.

Michael and the bikers studied each other in silence for a long moment. The girl and the youngster were with these four. Michael had known it from the moment he had turned the corner. They were her protection, he was sure of that, and maybe something else besides. Looking from one biker to the next, Michael didn't feel he was in any position to ask questions just now. But nobody had made a move against him. The four of them looked interested—a little surprised, maybe—but not really threatening. The blond fellow with a new-wave spike to his hair smiled at Michael. Michael smiled back.

The girl climbed on behind the blond and put her arms around his waist. The kid got on the next bike down the line, behind a serious Latin-looking guy with long dark hair.

The four revved their engines and took off up the street. Michael watched them go. The girl didn't even look behind.

"Hey!" his brother called to him. "Come on!"

Sam and his mother stood behind him, next to the Land Rover. Michael hadn't even heard his mother pull up.

What difference did it make, anyway? Whatever dreams he had were over, riding away behind the leader of a motorcycle gang. Michael would have to go home now. He paused before he turned away to take a final look.

The girl glanced back at him and smiled.

She had smiled at him! The motorcycles turned a corner and vanished from view. But that no longer mattered. The girl had smiled at him!

He walked back to join his mother and brother. He realized he had a stupid grin on his face. He didn't care.

"He met a girl," Sam remarked.

Their mother looked at her two sons. "I guess no one cares that I got a job."

"I do!" Sam piped up. "Congratulations, Mom!" He climbed into the passenger seat of the Rover. "Does that mean we can get a TV?"

Mom laughed. Michael got in the backseat. His mother and brother continued talking and laughing as they rode back to their grandfather's place. Michael heard the sound of their voices, but he paid no attention to the words. She had smiled that beautiful smile. What more did he need? Michael tilted his head back so that he could look up out of the rear window and count the summer stars.

Nine

The sun glinted fiercely off the sea and sand as it peeked over the mountains to the east. Michael never knew it could be this bright this early in the morning. Still, if he was going to make any money, he had to get a job, and this was the only job he knew of in Santa Carla.

He had seen the notice the night before, tacked to a telephone pole along the Boardwalk: "Dayworkers wanted. $4.00/hour." The notice had said to show up for work on the beach at seven A.M. From the crowd around him it looked like about thirty other people had read the notice too.

He wondered if there would be enough work for all these people. Some of the others had the half-starved look of teenage runaways; a few of them were older—drifters or drunks, probably. The rest were high-school kids like Michael. He thought he recognized a couple of them from last night's bonfires.

The crowd this morning was pretty quiet, especially after how noisy this beach had been last time Michael had walked down it. It was probably too early in the morning to talk. Michael squinted across the bright sand at the calm, morning ocean. His eyes wanted to close completely. If he was going to do this sort of thing day after day, he'd have to start getting more sleep.

He heard the rustle of bodies moving behind him. Somebody coughed. A couple others talked softly to each other. Michael glanced around. Those that had sprawled in the sand were standing. The crowd looked toward the Boardwalk. Three men climbed down from the wooden platform and approached them across the sand.

The man in the lead was tall and broad-shouldered and walked toward them with long strides that made the distance disappear. His skin was a deep brown, like his face had been carved from mahogany; his shirt was a pure white. The contrast between the two hurt Michael's eyes even more than looking at the sand. He wore a dark red tie but no jacket, and his collar button was undone to give room for his massive, muscular neck.

He was the man in charge. That was obvious from the moment the three of them had stepped off the Boardwalk. His two assistants ran across the sand to keep up with him. The one that kept falling behind carried a clipboard.

The boss paused just short of the crowd. He pulled a cigar from his pocket and lit it. "Too many of you today. Can't use all of you." He puffed on his cigar until it really started to burn. "Anybody I point out, give your name to John here. You're hired for the day."

He pulled the cigar from his mouth and used it as an extension of his fingers, singling out a dozen people in the crowd. Michael saw the cigar pointing at him. One of the assistants asked him who he was. They wrote his name down on the clipboard. That meant he was in! The assistant waved for Michael and a couple of the others to follow him.

Michael trudged across the beach, leaving the rest of the crowd behind. He never dreamed it was going to be this easy!

This was it. They had finally moved to the pits. There really was nothing to do in Santa Carla.

Sam kicked sand into the cracks as he shuffled along the Boardwalk. That's all there was here; sand, sand, and more sand. And when you were done with that, you could probably find even more sand. Santa Carla wasn't just the pits. It was the sand pits.

There were a bunch of people out on the beach, cleaning up the mess from last night's bonfires, loading cans and papers and bits of charred wood into oversize trash bags. Sam stepped to the edge of the Boardwalk to watch and realized that one of the cleaners was his brother.

Sam jumped down onto the sand and started toward Michael. Maybe he would have some decent ideas for things to do around here. Sam sighed. It showed him just how far his life had fallen when the best thing he could think of to do was go and talk with his brother.

Michael asked him how it was going.

"How is it going?" Sam replied. "There are no malls and no cineplexes in Santa Carla! I found out last night there was no MTV. Now, no brat-pack movies! I will never again know of anything hip that is happening anywhere!"

Michael laughed as he scooped up a pair of dented beer cans. "Why don't you go for a swim?"

Sam stared at his brother, too stunned to reply.

"Yeah," Michael repeated, "go for a swim. You know, like, before there were malls, there was like, the ocean?"

Sam turned and left without another word. He didn't know why he expected his brother to understand.

Still, what else was there to do around here? He could kill half an hour just going back to Grandpa's and putting on his suit.

So here it was, life in Santa Carla. Sam climbed back onto the Boardwalk and headed for the house. Pacific Ocean, here I come.

Why did they call these things "fun tubes," anyways?

Sam had gone back to the house and gotten his suit, then dutifully turned back to the beach. That was when he started to have second thoughts. And third and fourth thoughts, besides.

For one thing, Sam hadn't set foot in an ocean for years. He wasn't too big on swimming, either. Oh, they had done some basic stuff in the pool at school. But that was a small, enclosed, safe little bit of water with sides and a nice cement bottom. Sam's experience with larger bodies of water was just about nonexistent. His old hometown of Phoenix wasn't particularly big on lakes, let alone oceans. He'd heard all sorts of horror stories about how strong the waves were in the Pacific. And people were always warning you to "Watch out for the undertow!" And what about sharks?

Well, straight swimming was out then, at least for now. Sam walked back to the beach, anyway. He couldn't spend the rest of his life (as long and boring as it was going to be in Santa Carla) scared of the ocean. There had to be some way he could start out small in the Pacific.

That's when he saw the "fun tube" rental sign. Sam had no idea what a "fun tube" was, but taking something into the ocean with you sounded a lot safer than going into the water all by yourself.

He wasn't too sure about that now. The fun tube turned out to be nothing more than a big inner tube; well, a bright yellow inner tube with the words FUN TUBE stenciled in red on its side. Sam had forked over his dollar fifty for this thing; he figured he might as well give it a good try. He grabbed his sunglasses and comic book and headed for the waves.

Unfortunately the big yellow rubber fun tube seemed to have other ideas. Sam waded out in the shallows, then attempted to launch himself out over the waves. The fun tube immediately bounced up in his face. Sam threw his arm over the top of the thing. He thought he had it under control then, until the next wave, when the fun tube flipped completely over.

Sam rose sputtering from the depths, still clutching the fun tube. He would not be beaten by a stupid piece of rubber! He was going to stay out here until he learned to control it. He swore he wouldn't leave until he started having fun.

There was a great shout from back on the beach. Sam paddled the fun tube around to see half a dozen surfers running right at him.

What should he do? Sam didn't know enough about working this tube to keep it upright, much less get it out of somebody's way. Why were these characters coming this way? Couldn't they see him out here?

The surfers smiled as they caught up to him. One of the guys had a shaved head, another a Mohawk. It was the third guy, though, that really got Sam's attention.

He recognized this guy! There was no way he could forget that stupid haircut and bleached hair. It was the comic-book thief from last night. The Surf Nazi.

The Surf Nazi stopped to glare down at Sam. "Hey dude!" The thief laughed. "My beach, my wave!"

He grabbed Sam's fun tube and threw it, with Sam inside, back on shore.

Sam struggled to push the fun tube away and stand up. He could hear the surfers' laughter as they splashed out into the ocean.

This place was the pits.

He didn't know anybody could get this hot. Michael shaded his eyes from the glaring sun, scanning the beach for trash.

Before today, Michael had had no idea how much work was involved in keeping a beach clean. He had spent all morning cleaning up everything from broken bottles to dead fish from the sand dunes, then had to load all the garbage bags on trucks so that the trash could be taken to a dump. Now, after half an hour off for lunch, they had shown him to the other side of the pier and a brand-new beach, even more littered than the one he'd cleaned that morning. Michael had the feeling that after today he'd never want to see a beach again.

One thing was for sure. He knew he had never sweated so much in his life. His damp hair stuck to his forehead. He pushed it back with his hand, letting his eyes wander back over the Boardwalk.

Wasn't that her? A girl with bare shoulders and long curly hair was looking into a store window on just the other side of the Boardwalk. Michael wanted to call out, to get her to turn around. But he didn't even know her name.

She turned around, anyway. And it wasn't her.

It was just wishful thinking, then. The girl on the Boardwalk didn't look anything like her, really. This girl was shorter, her hair not quite the right color.

And why did Michael expect to ever see the girl from last night again? He had been thinking about her through the heat of the day. What had her smile meant, really? The euphoria of the night before had worn away, as if he had sweated it out by picking up bottles and lifting trash bags.

He really knew nothing about her. It was all just wishful thinking.

The girl that wasn't her walked on down the Boardwalk. Michael speared another crumpled paper cup and tossed it in his bag. The work was real, and the money would be real. He didn't want to be like the kids he saw that morning, sleeping out on the beach or under the Boardwalk, hungry and with no real place to go. Michael Emerson was going to go someplace. He would make sure of that. Whether or not he found the girl just didn't matter.

It was all just wishful thinking.

Somehow Lucy felt she should be more cheerful than this. Here she was, on the first day of a new job at Max's Video. The work was certainly pleasant enough. The cashier, Maria, had spent the first hour or so "showing her the ropes," as she had put it. After that, all Lucy had to do was refile videotapes and help an occasional customer. She told Maria she felt guilty doing so little. Maria just smiled and told her to wait for the weekends. "It all averages out," she had added.

So they had settled in for the afternoon. And once Lucy became more or less confident that she wouldn't make a complete fool of herself around the customers, she began to feel the slightest bit dissatisfied.

And just what was wrong, Lucy Emerson? The answer was obvious, although she had probably spent the better part of the afternoon ignoring it.

She had looked forward to seeing Max again. She had been disappointed when he wasn't there when the store opened but decided that feeling was nothing more than new-job jitters. She hadn't realized how truly strong her feelings were until it dawned on her that he wasn't coming in. It was simple, really. Lucy Emerson was acting like some sort of love-struck schoolgirl.

She tried to ignore it and pass the time talking with her coworker. Somehow the conversation turned to their boss.

"You know, I'd be out on the street if it wasn't for Max." Maria laughed softly and shook her perfectly coiffed head. "Nobody would have given me a job the way I looked when I walked in here."

"Where is he, anyway?" Lucy asked, hoping she sounded casual. "I haven't see him all day."

"Didn't he tell you?" Maria frowned as she studied her perfect nails. Whatever she found wrong with them was completely beyond Lucy. "He only comes in here nights. He's busy opening another store in Los Gatos. It's going to be much bigger than this one."

Another store in Los Gatos? So Max wasn't just good-looking. He was successful too. Hold yourself back, Lucy. Remember how all your friends back in Phoenix warned you about falling for someone on the rebound so soon after your divorce? You really don't know very much about Max. Take your time, girl, she told herself. Get to know him better. Then you can fall for him.

She heard a motor and the beep of a motorcycle horn. She looked out the window and saw her sons pull up on Michael's Honda. She asked Maria if it was all right to go out and see them. Maria said anything was fine with her.

Sam jumped off the bike as Lucy opened the door.

"See you later!" Michael called.

Where was he off to now? She was hoping her whole family could get together that evening and talk.

"Michael?" she replied. "I get off in another twenty minutes. I thought maybe we'd all get a bite together."

Her son shifted uncomfortably in his seat. "I've got plans," he murmured. He pulled a battered envelope from his pants pocket. "Here."

"What's this?" Lucy opened the envelope to find a folded Christmas card with a half dozen folded five- and ten-dollar bills inside.

"Take it," Michael answered. "It's some money I had left over from Christmas . . ." He paused, then added, "And some I earned today."

"He's a garbageman," Sam offered helpfully.

Lucy shook her head and handed the envelope back.

"No thanks, Michael. You'll need this when you go back to school."

Her son stared at the envelope in her hand for a long moment, then grabbed and pocketed it at last. He waved to Lucy and Sam as he gunned the motorcycle and took off down the street.

So her son wanted to help support the family. Lucy smiled. What a nice thing to do! She shouldn't worry about Michael. Not when he could make a gesture like that. All his problems probably came from trying too hard. Losing a father, even through divorce, must be awfully hard on someone his age. In a way, then, Michael was trying to take his father's place, to become the family provider. It was sweet but totally unnecessary. Now that she had a job, everything was going to work out fine. How could she let him know that she was perfectly happy if he just stayed what he was; an average, hardworking teenage boy?

One thing was certain. For the first time all day she was really happy.

Ten

Michael smiled as he looked at himself in the mirror. This was all right. He was glad his mother made him keep the money, after all.

He squared his shoulders and frowned at his reflection, tugging the battered black leather sleeves until they were just right. This jacket made him look years older. Michael smiled and shoved his hands in the jacket pockets. With this jacket on, he belonged on a motorcycle. Those teenagers last night had nothing on him anymore. He told the shop girl with the spiky pink hair that he'd take it.

He walked out onto the Boardwalk a new man. Let those bikers mess with him now. He'd take them on anytime. He glanced at himself in the store windows as he walked. Not bad, Emerson, not bad. Maybe he'd cut his hair just a little bit weirder and get a new pair of jeans.

A sign in the next window read EARS PIERCED: $10.

Michael stopped and considered the sign. Why not? Those guys he met last night did it. He checked the envelope in his pocket to see if he still had enough.

"It's a rip-off."

Michael spun around at the sound of the girl's voice.

She smiled at him. That smile, that face, that hair, those shoulders. For a second he couldn't believe what his eyes were telling him.

It was her.

He smiled back carefully, trying not to break into a goofy grin. He wanted his face to be as cool as his new jacket.

But what should he say?

"Hi," he managed at last.

She frowned a bit and glanced at the side of his head. "If you want your ear pierced, I'll do it."

Michael didn't know what to say.

She turned and walked down the Boardwalk. Michael hurried to catch up. He couldn't blow this now. This was his chance to get to know her!

"What's your name?" he asked as soon as he reached her side.

She smiled at him again. "Star."

Star? Well, he shouldn't be surprised.

"Oh," he answered. "Your folks, too, huh?"

Now it was her turn to be surprised. She looked at him with her big beautiful eyes.

"What do you mean?"

He laughed. "Ex-hippies. I came this close to being called Moon Child or Moonbeam or something." He looked back into her wide eyes. Her face was only inches away.

"But Star's great," he added after a moment. "I like Star."

She smiled the sweetest smile that Michael had ever seen. "Me too."

"I'm Michael," he added.

Star nodded her head. "Michael's great. I like Michael."

Michael found himself smiling as well. She was teasing him. That was fine with him.

He didn't know what to say next.

Star broke the silence a moment later.

"I guess you're new around here."

Michael shrugged. "Sort of. We used to come here summers when I was a kid. Now we're here on a permanent basis."

Her smile broadened even more. She must like him too! Michael couldn't believe his good luck.

But what should he say to her next? He couldn't exactly ask her out, right here and now. Could he?

"Are you hungry?" he asked after a second. "Want to get something to eat?"

"Okay," she replied.

This was going even better than he expected. But where to go? He had passed a neat-looking pizza joint on his way down the main road to the Boardwalk. It meant a short ride on his bike. Was that okay with her?

Star said it was fine. They walked together out to the parking area. Michael decided he liked it with her walking by his side. He hoped that sometime soon he could hold her hand.

Four motorcycles turned from the beach road onto the Boardwalk. Their engines roared as they approached Michael and Star. Even in the darkness Michael recognized them. It was the bikers from last night.

"The Lost Boys," Star told him.

The one with the punk blond hair pulled close to Star.

"Where are you going?"

"For a ride," she replied curtly.

The Lost Boy looked at Michael. His face wasn't angry. If anything, it was amused.

"With him?"

"Yeah," she answered, looking away.

The Lost Boy gunned his bike. It was a Triumph, a machine big enough to make Michael's Honda look like a toy. He eased up, letting the engine rev back down.

He smiled at Michael.

"I'm David." He pointed, one by one, to the other three.

"Paul—" He indicated the boy farthest away, with a broad face and long blonde hair.

"Dwayne—" The fellow with the long face and jet black hair to his shoulders stared silently at Michael. The kid Star had been with the night before sat behind him.

"Marco." The skinny guy with curly brown hair and the embroidered jacket nodded.

"Hi!" The young kid waved from behind Dwayne. He was wearing a deep blue military jacket, the old-fashioned kind the Beatles wore on the *Sgt. Pepper* album. He smiled and brushed the hair from his face. "I'm Laddie!"

"This is Michael," Star added.

Nobody said anything for a minute. Michael realized they were all watching him. What did they expect?

Well, if they wanted him to make the first move, he'd be glad to oblige. Michael walked over to his own bike. He turned to Star. "We still going?"

"Honda 250, huh?" David asked.

"That's right," Michael replied. Were they going to make fun of his bike now?

"C'mon, Star." David nodded to the girl, twisting his head toward the seat behind him. "Climb on."

"Star?" Michael began.

She looked at Michael with a sweet, sad smile, then climbed on behind David.

David grinned in Michael's direction. Michael wished he could push in David's teeth.

"Know where Hudson's Bluff is? Overlooking the point?" David gunned the Triumph again.

Michael realized that this was a challenge. And there were four of them on their massive, customized street bikes against him with his little Honda. But David had taken Star away, just as she and Michael were getting to know each other.

Michael wanted her back.

He kicked back the bike's kickstand and threw his leg over the seat. He started up the Honda, the smaller engine's roar lost beneath the noise of David's bike.

He stared at David. Michael was ready.

"You don't have to beat me, Michael," David said, still grinning. "Just try to keep up."

David took off with a yell, followed by the other Lost Boys. Michael took off, too, shifting up quickly and pushing the throttle as far as he dared, just to keep up with them.

David turned his bike away from the main road, straight down the Boardwalk. Michael realized David was leading them to the beach.

They hit the main part of the Boardwalk at full speed. People ran out of their way, cursing them as they passed. Michael had to swerve to miss an elderly couple. He wondered if scaring pedestrians was David's idea of a good time. But then David turned, bouncing his bike down the broad, wooden steps that ended on the beach. The Lost Boys were right behind him.

Well, if that's what they wanted, that's what they were going to get. Michael clenched his teeth as he steered the Honda down the stairs. The lurching motion threatened to rip the handlebars from his grip, but he held on to follow the others as their wheels sprayed sand. David was weaving his way through the evening bonfires, revving his engine as he went. People stared as they passed. It wasn't as crowded out here as it was up on the Boardwalk, though, and people were staying out of their way. Michael could concentrate on catching up with the others.

The Lost Boys yelled to each other up ahead as they weaved their bikes in and out of the surf. They probably did this sort of thing all the time. They were having a great time. Michael wished he could say the same. It was all he could do to stay close enough to make it look like a race. He was glad, though, that they had left the bonfires behind. He had had visions of losing control of his bike and ramming headlong into either the crowd or the flames. It was easier going out here at the edge of the surf.

Then he realized they were headed for the underside of the pier. There was a lot of weight on that pier with all the shops and restaurants, and the platform was supported by huge wooden pilings, each one maybe four feet across. The pilings were close together, too, with only maybe a couple of yards between each. The whole thing reminded Michael of a dense forest, with the platform of the pier where the leaves should have been.

David was heading straight for it. Well, Michael thought, at least he could catch up when David slowed down to get through those pilings.

Instead, as David got closer, he sped up.

This was suicide! Michael skidded on the sand and slowed his Honda down.

The Lost Boys screamed as one and sped into the space between the pilings. As soon as you got away from the bonfires, it was pretty dark out here in the dunes. But there was no light at all under the pier. It looked like the inside of a cave.

The last set of taillights winked as the fourth bike raced behind the pilings. Michael would lose them if he waited any longer. He still had to follow them in.

He could see the gang in front of him, doing hairpin turns across the tree trunks, speeding back and forth, crisscrossing each other's paths. David cut off Paul, who barely avoided Marco as he rode close behind Dwayne. Somehow they weren't running into each other or the pilings. Somehow they weren't all dead.

Then Michael saw the light of bonfires up ahead between the last of the pilings. They were all going to make it through this alive.

The bikes came out on the other side of the pier. The beach changed up here. It was no longer flat but rolled in gentle dunes. There were fewer bonfires out here, too, one large one nearby and a couple smaller fires in the distance. Michael guessed that this part of the beach was too far from the main action.

David rode his bike to the base of the biggest dune, just beyond the main bonfire, pausing for the others to join

him. Michael was the last to pull up. Was it time for more
fancy tricks? This didn't look like Hudson's Bluff, the
place David had mentioned when he issued his challenge.
Well, Michael had kept up with the rest of them so far.
Where could they go that would be worse than driving
through those pilings under the pier?

David gunned his cycle and took off straight up and off
the top of the dune, flying through the air right into the
bonfire.

David landed on the other side. He spun his bike around
and stopped to wait for the others.

Marco went next, accelerating up the hill and out into
space, plunging through air and fire to land next to David.
Paul and Dwayne followed quickly. Paul's takeoff from
the dune was fast and high, but Dwayne was a little bit
slower than the others. He screamed as he fell through the
air toward the fire. Michael thought for sure that Dwayne
would land in the flames.

He landed at the edge of the burning wood and went to
join the others.

Now it was Michael's turn.

If he decided to do it. He had come this far on the Lost
Boys' joyride. That should prove he could take it. He kept
up with the others off the Boardwalk, over the beach, and
through the pilings. Just how far did they expect him to
go?

The Lost Boys watched him from the other side of the
fire. Dwayne almost fell into that fire. Why should Michael risk his neck for a stupid challenge like this?

He saw Star watching him from the back of David's bike.
Even at this distance he thought he saw her smile.

That made it worth his while, after all. He'd prove to
Star that he was as good as David or any of the Lost
Boys. All four of them had gotten safely through the
flames, after all. David's trick was probably one of those
showy stunts that looked a lot more dangerous than it

actually was. That had to be it. Why else would all four of them have jumped through the bonfire, especially when a couple of them were carrying a girl and a ten-year-old boy?

Well, it was his turn now. Michael revved his engine and took off as fast as he could. His bike was smaller than the others. He'd have to push the Honda as far as he could. If he was any slower than Dwayne, he would land in the fire. He didn't want to think what would happen to him then.

He cleared the sand dune in half a second. Michael felt his wheels leave the ground. He felt more like he was floating in air than falling, like he was some sort of butterfly being drawn toward the bonfire's flames. The fire rushed to meet him. He closed his eyes.

He opened them a second later to find the ground rapidly approaching. He felt the bike leaning to one side as the back wheel hit the sand. He didn't want to fall, not now! He shifted his weight as the front wheel came down and gunned the cycle forward. The bike righted itself, and he rode to join the Lost Boys.

All of them smiled at him now. Still, the best smile of all came from Star.

Michael remembered to breathe. David laughed and took off on his bike with the others close behind.

What else could Michael do but follow?

Eleven

This was getting better and better.

After they left Santa Carla, David had waved for Michael to bring his bike up and ride next to him. Michael figured he must have passed his initiation. It was a beautiful night, late enough so that the five cycles had the back roads they traveled on all to themselves. David led them over a trestle. Michael glanced to his right and saw the ocean in the distance, the surf crashing against tumbled rocks. They must be coming out to the bluff David had talked about.

Once off the trestle, they turned onto a dirt road that led toward the ocean. David pulled a bit ahead, and Michael found Star by his side, her long hair blowing in the wind. She twisted her head to look at him and smiled, then reached out her hand toward his.

Michael shifted his weight on his bike and put his own hand out. They touched for a long moment. The warmth of her fingers felt electric against his palm.

Then Star's hand was gone. David turned to Michael and shouted loud enough to be heard over the cycles and the wind.

"*Now* we race!"

He grinned and was gone. Michael took off after him. His eyes were on the bike ahead of him, but his thoughts were all of Star. There was something special to her touch. He had to touch her again, to hold her hand, to softly stroke her cheek, and more. There was so much more.

They were out on the bluff now, high above the ocean.

There was a sheer cliff to Michael's right. It was hard to tell in the moonlight, but he guessed there might be as much as a five-hundred-foot drop to the rocks below.

Where was David going so fast? The cliff looked like it swung around in front of them up ahead. Still, Michael did his best to keep up. He was sure David knew what he was doing.

No! David was heading straight for the cliff! There was no way he could stop in time. He would kill himself, with Star and Michael thrown in for a bonus. This wasn't like jumping through a bonfire. They would fly off the cliff and crash into the rocks hundreds of feet below.

Michael braked as hard as he could, gripping the handlebars as if he might somehow pull the bike back from the cliff. The bike swerved. He could feel the wheels going out from under him. He was going too fast. He had to stay with it. David braked next to him as the cliff edge rushed toward them. David had stopped, his front wheel at the edge of the drop.

But Michael's bike was still moving. The cliff was just ahead. Michael threw his weight to one side.

He slid to a stop, his front wheel still spinning out over the edge of the cliff.

Michael pulled his bike back onto the bluff. Then he started to shake. He heard the other Lost Boys arrive, but it was as if they were ten miles away rather than ten feet, the sounds of their engines barely penetrating Michael's shock.

Then the shakes were gone, as suddenly as they had arrived. Michael looked up at David, who climbed off his bike as if nothing had happened.

That was it. Michael felt an overwhelming fury grow inside him, a fury that had a single focus. He rushed over to David and punched him in the face.

Everyone was silent. Michael was suddenly aware of the waves crashing on the cliffs below. Star's head was turned, looking at Laddie. Everyone else watched Michael. Michael waited, steeling himself against David's answering blow.

Instead David smiled a big, broad grin.

"How far are you willing to go, Michael?"

He turned, and the other Lost Boys followed.

Whatever she did, it was going to turn out wrong.

Star looked down at Laddie, away from David and Michael. She was afraid that if she turned back to the two of them, she would start to cry.

Why did it have to be this way? Too much had happened, too much had changed. She knew she couldn't go back to her parents; not after what happened. The only family she had anymore was Laddie; even though they weren't really related, she thought of him as a little brother. Until yesterday that had been enough.

She had thought her feelings were dead. Oh, there was David, and the other Lost Boys, too, but that was different. Star had known that from the start. She was alone now. She wanted to be alone.

Then she had seen Michael.

There was something about Michael, something special.

She had been confused at first. When the Lost Boys had picked her up from the Boardwalk last night, she didn't even want to talk about her newfound feelings. Somehow, though, David had known something had changed. There had been nothing to do then but to tell him. To her surprise David had encouraged it.

Then David told her his reasons, and she wasn't surprised anymore. Oh, Michael! You should stay away from the gangs in Santa Carla.

Michael didn't know what he was getting into. She didn't know how she could tell him, either. If she said the wrong thing, he'd run away and she'd never see him again.

It had all gone much too far. If only she'd known when this had all started, there might have been some way—

Star caught herself falling too deep into self-pity. She'd known enough about what she was getting into, even from the first. Maybe there hadn't been that many choices after she left home, but she had gotten herself into this thing. And Laddie too. It wasn't so bad. Until now she thought she had accepted it.

Then there was Michael. What exactly did she want from him? Was she looking for a white knight to get her out?

She was afraid, when he hit David, that Michael might not live long enough to do anything. But David didn't hit Michael back. David smiled instead and asked Michael just how far he would go.

In a way that might be even worse.

But Michael was still here. They could still have time together. Maybe she could find a way to tell him everything, to change her life and start out fresh. She knew, really, that he couldn't be her savior. Life wasn't like that; that sort of thing only happened in movies and books. But maybe they could work together. Maybe, even without white knights, there was a way out for both of them.

Michael had no idea there were places like this around Santa Carla. It was beautiful up here on the edge of the bluff with the ocean crashing far below. He wished Star and he could be here all alone, without any of the others.

Maybe they'd be able to come up here later, just the two of them. For now they had all become part of David's expedition, walking along a cliffside path in the moonlight.

Then David stepped off the cliff, onto a set of rotting, rickety stairs. The railings above the top steps were covered with official-looking signs. CONDEMNED! they read in gigantic boldface type. UNSAFE! UNLAWFUL TO GO PAST THIS POINT!

David started down the stairs. Star and the other Lost
Boys followed. Michael had gone this far. David might be
a bit of a daredevil, but Michael was sure he wasn't a fool.
David always knew exactly what he was doing and how
much risk was involved.

The wind whipped off the ocean far below, blowing
Michael's hair in his face. The last of the Lost Boys
disappeared down the steps. If he was going, he had to do
it now. If they were all taking the stairs, Michael would
take them too.

The old wood complained under his boots. He tried not
to look down. If one of these stairs gave way, he had a
long way to go before he hit the rocks. He could hear
David and the others below. They were out of sight. He
had to hurry or he would lose them. He moved as quickly
as he dared, almost mechanically, putting one foot down,
then his other foot on the step below, then the first foot to
the step below that, back and forth, so that the rhythm of
his descent took on a life of its own and he no longer had
to think about just how high he was or where he had to
fall.

Star laughed, just ahead. He looked up, startled that she
might be that close. The cliff face behind him was in total
darkness, the rest of the sky a midnight blue, littered with
stars. It was so incredible that he forgot for a moment that
he was afraid. The stars were everywhere, the sea a distant
white below. He felt as if he were walking across the sky.

He had caught up with the others; they were just below.
He followed them as they climbed down another half
dozen twists and turns in the ancient stairs, past another
dozen • warning signs. The stairs stopped at the rocks,
boulders the size of houses that must have fallen down
from above. David led his party across the jumble of
stone, heading for an opening up ahead.

Michael had climbed around this kind of beach before.
He kept up easily with the others.

He stopped when he came to the opening of the cave. David smiled and waved at him to come inside.

The other Lost Boys lit a pair of hurricane lanterns as they walked inside. And the moonlight shone down through cracks in the ceiling, making the middle of the cave almost as bright as day.

But it was more than a cave. There was a house in here. No, it was bigger than that. Michael looked around in awe. It looked like some sort of old-fashioned hotel. The cave led right into the lobby.

This place was special. He knew it the moment he had looked into the cave. And it was the Lost Boys' place; he knew that too. Now they had brought him here. It might have taken a punch on David's jaw, but it looked like the Lost Boys had accepted Michael at last.

Where did this place come from? The floor wasn't quite level, and it slanted quite a bit to one side. But the whole thing was still covered by a thick carpet that was sort of a deep brownish-purple. There was a massive front desk made of dark wood, the kind you saw in old movies with the big guest register sitting open across the desktop. Next to the desk was a standing lamp with a huge lampshade covered in fringe and an overstuffed chair with small bits of white lace over the armrests and the top.

Michael was fascinated by those tiny bits of white. What did you call them? Doilies, that was it. He had seen them made out of paper. The ones on the chair looked like they were made out of cloth. Michael had never seen anything so delicate. He cautiously reached out to pick up the doily on the chair's headrest, but it crumbled where his fingers touched it and left a coating of fine white dust on his hand.

There was a painting of some sort that took up an entire wall. It looked like some sort of old-time summer resort scene, but the moonlight filtering in from the cracks overhead wasn't bright enough for Michael to make out details.

David stood in front of a tall, wrought-iron gate. Michael realized that once that gate must have held the hotel elevator.

David smiled at Michael's surprise. "This was the hottest resort in Santa Carla, back about eighty years ago. Too bad they built it right on top of the San Andreas Fault."

He laughed and walked behind the long front desk. "In 1906, when the big one hit San Francisco, the ground opened up and this place took a header into the crack." He opened his arms wide to include the whole lobby. "Now it's ours."

Paul slapped Michael on the back. "Man, you wouldn't believe the cool stuff we've found down here!"

But Michael could believe it easily. This was an incredible place! He smiled over at Star.

Star didn't smile back. Was something wrong?

"Come on, Michael," she said quietly. She seemed a little nervous. "I want to go."

"No." David stepped between them. He was still smiling. "Stick around."

Part of Michael wanted to do just that, to take some time and explore this neat old hotel. This was a great place, but it made Star unhappy for some reason. And he was only here, really, to be with Star. If she didn't want to stay here, Michael knew, then he didn't want to, either.

Maybe she wanted to get away to be alone with Michael. The thought sent a chill from his shoulders straight down to his groin. He looked past David to Star. Her eyes were pleading for him to take her away.

"Uh—" he began. "We were gonna grab some food."

"Good idea!" David replied. "Marco! Food!"

Marco nodded and left the way they had come in.

"See?" David said. "All you gotta do is ask."

Michael shrugged in Star's direction. The Lost Boys had invited them to dinner. They had to stick around for a little while now. They'd still be able to leave soon enough.

David pulled a joint from his shirt pocket and lit it.

"How about an appetizer?" He took a drag from the joint and passed it to Michael.

Michael looked at the burning cigarette in his hand. Heck. He might as well. Still, he wished he could get Star alone for a minute so that the two of them could talk.

He looked over toward her, hoping to catch her eye, but she had already turned away.

Twelve

VAMPIRES EVERYWHERE.

What a title. Real subtle. Sam lay back on his bed and glanced critically at the cover of his most recent purchase.

It was a real product of the early fifties, before the comics code showed up to take all the blood and violence away from comic books. The cover showed a young guy, not much older than Sam, driving a stake through this vampire's heart. The young guy was smiling in triumph, but he shouldn't have been. Just behind him, out of his sight but about to jump on him, were three more vampires, their fangs dripping blood. The whole thing was drawn in that slightly cartoony style popular back then, sort of like Jack Davis or Harvey Kurtzman. It was still pretty creepy. In the lower right-hand corner was a small yellow box with the words: "Can anyone survive THE NIGHT OF THE BLOODSUCKERS?"

Sam opened the comic to the first page. There was a drawing of a tall, distinguished-looking vampire, sort of like John Carradine in *House of Dracula*. He stared off the page at Sam, a word balloon emerging from his fanged and smiling mouth to introduce the story.

"Welcome, gentle reader, to another tasty sampling of vampire tales. And I do mean tasty. It's time now for a shaggy-dog story of a different kind. How different? Well, you could say the mutt in our story was a real *bloodhound*, if you know what I mean. You'll never look at the family pooch quite the same once you've finished "HOUNDS OF HELL!"

"Ten o'clock!" His mother stuck her head in the door. "Lights out!"

Sam put the comic down. Why did his mother have to yell like that? He had almost had a heart attack!

His mother walked across the room, oblivious to the damage she had done. She opened his closet and hung up a couple of Sam's shirts. She turned away and walked over toward the light switch.

But she had left the closet door open. First the shout, and now this. It was really too much.

"Mom!" Sam complained.

She looked behind her and made a *tsk*ing sound with her tongue. She walked back and closed the offending door.

"You're right," she said, facing Sam. "I can't sleep with the closet door open, either. Not even a crack." She walked over toward the bed. "Your father never minded, though. It could be wide open for all he cared."

She nodded to herself. "I think one of the reasons I divorced him was because he never believed"—she stepped closer, her voice hushed—"in the horror"—she was right by the bed now, her voice no more than a whisper—"of the *closet monster!*"

"Closet monster?" a deep voice intoned.

Sam and his mother screamed as one.

"Dad!" Mom yelled. "Don't sneak up on people like that!"

Grandpa smiled from where he stood in the doorway. "It's called the Indian walk." He pointed to his moccasins by way of explanation. "Walkin' without makin' a sound."

He stepped into the room. Sam saw he was hiding something behind his back.

Grandpa smiled and winked in Sam's direction. "Brought you a little somethin' to dress up your room with, Sam.

He pulled the surprise from behind his back. It was a stuffed woodchuck. It was also the ugliest stuffed woodchuck Sam had ever seen, raised on its hind legs, with bulging eyes and big buck teeth.

Sam looked to his mother, but she shot back a glance that told him he was on his own. Sam tried to smile. How could he react to a present like this?

Grandpa placed the woodchuck in a place of honor on the middle of Sam's dresser.

"Gee," Sam said after a moment. "Thanks, Grandpa."

Grandpa shook his head proudly, as if no thanks were needed.

"And remember," he added, "there's lots more where he came from."

His mother and grandfather walked to the door.

"Lights out, Sam," his mother ordered.

Sam looked down at the book in his hands. "Soon as I finish this comic. Okay, Mom?"

His mother relented with a smile and a nod. She shut the door behind her.

Sam felt an immense sense of relief. This was why he never read horror stuff. Once he started one of these things, he had to finish it. He wouldn't be able to sleep until he found out everything came out all right in the end.

Lucy shivered. It seemed unseasonably cold tonight. She walked down the hall to the thermostat and nudged the temperature up to seventy.

Her father walked up next to her.

"So how you doin'?"

"Okay, I guess." She gave him what she felt must be a tired smile. Did he really want to talk? With her father it was so hard to tell. Maybe she should talk to him about Max.

Grandpa regarded her in silence, an elderly hippie sphinx.

She decided not to tell him anything, at least for now. Instead she added, "Things are moving so fast on this planet, it takes nerves of steel just to be neurotic."

Grandpa nodded his head. "How's the job?"

Lucy shrugged. Maybe her father did want to talk, after all. "It's a job."

Another nod. "How's your boss?"

"Max?" So he had come up in conversation, anyway. Lucy tried to keep the interest out of her voice. "Oh, do you know him?"

"Let's just say I got my eye on him." Grandpa nodded and turned away. He walked down the hall to the stairs, leaving Lucy alone.

What did that mean? She wanted to call after him, to get him to explain. Sometimes her father could be so exasperating. He always had a comment on every man she had ever met! She remembered how much trouble she used to have bringing boys home when she was a teenager. She hoped she never ran her boys' lives the way her father used to try to run hers.

But "I've got my eye on him"? Just what was he trying to say? Maybe her father wanted to start running her life all over again.

"Bowser was just an old dog, like any other dog. He wasn't any particular breed, either. More likely he was a mixture of five or six. But if Bowser did have one thing special about him, it was his curiosity!"

The picture below the caption showed a mangy brown mutt sniffing at a rosebush. Sam turned the page of the comic book.

"But there were some things it was better not to be curious about, like that old house up on the hill!"

This wasn't working. Sam kept having the feeling he was being watched. He peeked over the top of the comic book.

Two eyes stared back at him. Woodchuck eyes. Artificial, brown-glass woodchuck eyes.

So that was it. Sam went back to reading his comic.

The dog kept wanting to explore the old house, but his master would keep him away, always walking Bowser on a leash. There was a picture of Bowser straining to get into the house. His master pulled the leash back, yelling, "No, Bowser! Not in there!"

The next panel began: "But then Bowser's leash broke!"

Sam couldn't stand it. He felt like the woodchuck's eyes were boring right through the comic. He put the book down and stared at the thing. He was being silly. The woodchuck glared back at him, baring his big yellow teeth. Sam tried to go back to the comic.

"Bowser barked, but it did no good. His master was gone!"

It was no good. Sam knew he was being silly. It didn't make any difference. Sam jumped out of bed, grabbed the woodchuck, and threw it in the closet.

He went back to reading.

"What had Bowser found? It smelled something like another dog, but it smelled more like dead things Bowser had sometimes found by the side of the road—"

There was a picture of a giant dog, blood dripping from its fangs.

This was more like it! Sam settled in to finish his story, comfortable at last.

Thirteen

This was all right. Michael wondered why he ever worried about these guys in the first place.

He slouched back in one of the old, overstuffed chairs. It was the softest chair he had ever felt. Rock and roll pounded from a ghetto blaster at the center of the room. The music surrounded Michael. He felt like he had on the Boardwalk the night before, only even more so. The music was in every move he made. The rhythm moved his muscles; the melody flowed in his blood. He was the music, and the music was fine.

The other Lost Boys were spread around the lobby on the other chairs and couches, except for Dwayne, who was doing some incredible moves with his skateboard in the entranceway, just in front of Michael.

Michael could watch Dwayne on that skateboard for hours. Maybe he already had. He had no idea how long he had been here. Wasn't Marco coming with the food? Michael wished he'd hurry up. He was starving.

He suddenly thought of Star. Where was she? He hadn't seen her for a while. Had she left? She was the whole reason he had come here, after all. Well, most of the reason. He couldn't let David get the better of him. Even if he did ride that monster of a Triumph. Still, David wasn't such a bad guy. Michael wondered if he would ever have enough money to get a Triumph. But where was Star? And how about Marco? God, he was starving. Michael shook his head. That grass was good, but it kind of snuck up on you. He could use the food to clear his head.

Michael sat up and blinked. He had to figure out where Star had gone. He had to figure out just what was going on here.

The room spun around him. He had to come down slow from this stuff. If he concentrated, he could sit up. He wasn't sure if he could walk. He didn't want to fall over before he took his first step. That would never do. He didn't want everybody laughing at him. Especially now, when the whole gang seemed to accept him.

Michael blinked again and took a deep breath. Maybe if he talked some, it would bring him farther out of it.

Michael looked around at the others. He opened his mouth. His voice sounded like it came from a long way off.

"Where are you guys from?"

Paul looked up from his couch and smiled dreamily.

"We're from right here."

Michael shook his head. No, they didn't understand. He wasn't making himself clear.

"I mean," he said, trying again, "where do you live?"

Dwayne laughed from his skateboard.

"Right here!" he shouted.

Michael frowned. This wasn't working out right. Maybe he could say it another way.

"Where are your people?"

Paul looked at the other Lost Boys. "Is he talking 'parents'?"

Dwayne laughed again. "What are *they*?"

That made them all laugh. What was going on here?

David stood up from his chair at the far side of the desk. "We do what we want, Michael. We have complete freedom." He took a step toward Michael's chair. "Nobody knows about this place. And nobody knows about us!"

Nobody knows? Michael stared at David. What was that supposed to mean?

"Freedom, Michael." David answered the question Michael had never asked. "No people. No rules."

He smiled as he approached. Michael found David's hand on his arm. "Want to be our brother, Michael?"

"Chow time!"

Marco walked into the room, toting a big brown bag with handles. He set the take-out food in front of David.

"Chinese!" David crowed. "Good choice!"

He pulled a white carton from the bag. Still smiling, he handed it to Michael with a flourish.

"Guests first!" he added.

Michael accepted it uncertainly. What was this about being their brother? Did they want him to join the gang? This was all happening so fast. He was having trouble thinking.

"Something wrong?" David asked.

Michael looked down at the carton he held in his hands. Nothing seemed right now. How could he tell them what he was feeling?

"It's only rice," David added. "Don't you like rice? Three hundred million Chinese people can't be wrong."

The carton felt much too heavy in his hand. The cardboard was rough and cold against his fingers. It was the grass. It was warping everything he felt, everything he heard, everything he said. It was only rice, after all. For a moment it had seemed much too heavy for rice. It was the grass, and this old hotel, and the Lost Boys. Michael was afraid he was getting paranoid. Sometimes things seemed really strange when David started to talk.

David had turned away and was busy handing cartons out to the others. Michael looked down to the rice he held in his hands. David had stuck a plastic spoon into the top of the carton. That was nice of him. It would make it easier. Michael was hungry.

Michael managed to get a big spoonful of rice into his mouth. The rice was hard and chewy against his teeth. It would take the edge off his hunger, though. He swallowed some and wondered if they had something around here to drink.

David turned back to him with a smile.

"So how do you like those maggots, Michael?"

"What?" Michael replied. What was David talking about?

David tapped the side of Michael's carton with his index finger. "You're eating maggots. How do they taste?"

Michael looked down at the inside of the carton he held in his hands.

The rice was moving.

No. David was right. It wasn't rice. It was maggots. The carton was full of tiny, white, sluglike things, blindly crawling over each other, climbing up the spoon.

Michael dropped the carton. He didn't want those shiny, white things touching him.

Then he remembered he had eaten some of them. He could feel them crawling across his teeth and tongue, pushing their round, white bodies between his lips. They would crawl from his mouth to cover his face! He spat out what remained in his mouth, using his fingers to pry free the last few that had squirmed between his teeth.

Michael gagged. He had swallowed some of them! He wanted to vomit. He stared down at the floor where the carton had fallen on its side. Some of the white had spilled out on the floor. It wasn't moving. It was only rice.

The Lost Boys were all laughing. Suddenly Star was next to him.

"Leave him alone!"

David smiled and shook his head. "Sorry, Michael. No hard feelings, huh?" He handed Michael another carton. "Here. Try these noodles."

Michael accepted the carton with some trepidation. What was going on here? David and the Lost Boys were playing games. Maybe it was some sort of initiation stunt. Michael wished he hadn't gotten so stoned. Maybe eating a few noodles would make him feel better.

Michael looked down in the carton.

The noodles were moving too.

A hundred squiggling flatworms oozed around each other, their oily skins glistening brown and blue in the bright moonlight.

David asked him what was wrong.

"Worms!" Michael replied in disgust.

David took the carton back.

"Worms?" he repeated. He smiled as he lifted the carton to his lips. He tilted his head back and slowly began to pour the contents of the carton into his mouth. Large blue worms wriggled between his lips and flopped against his tongue.

What was David doing? Michael grabbed the other boy's arm. "Don't! Stop!"

"Why?" David smiled and pushed the carton toward Michael. "They're only noodles."

Michael had to fight back his growing revulsion before he looked into the white box David held. But nothing was moving. There were only noodles.

The Lost Boys laughed long and hard.

"That's enough!" Star demanded. She took Michael's arm and pulled him toward her.

"Star," he said. It was good that she was here. A new song came on the radio. Dwayne turned it up loud. Michael looked at Star. He realized he was smiling too much. He didn't care.

The others were moving to the song. Star took his hand and pulled him to a spot away from the others in the middle of the lobby. She moved back and forth to the song. She wanted to dance! Michael followed her as best as he could without getting too dizzy. He could dance with Star for the rest of time.

David walked toward them. He was carrying a bottle of wine. Something to drink at last! He poured some into a paper cup and offered it to Michael.

Star grabbed Michael's wrist to keep him from drinking.

David looked at the two of them. He pointed the bottle toward Michael.

"You want to be one of us, huh?"

"Don't, Michael!" Star whispered urgently. "You don't have to. It's blood."

Michael looked down at the cup in his hand.

So he'd been right all along. This was an initiation, and he bet this was the final step. And Star was in on it too. Well, he shouldn't be surprised. She and Michael had just barely met. She had known David and the others for a lot longer than that.

He smiled at David. He knew what they were doing. First the maggots, then the worms, now this. How much of a fool did they think he was?

The wine really was as dark as blood. It was the best joke of all. He lifted the cup to his lips. He'd show David and the others that he wasn't afraid of anything.

"Good joke," he said. "Blood."

They all watched him drink it. It was salty and sour for wine. Michael wondered where David had found it. It probably had been down in this cave ever since the earthquake.

A bit of the wine trickled from the corner of his mouth. He wiped it away with the back of his hand. It was such a dark red, the same color as the carpet beneath his feet, the color of dried blood.

The room was spinning around him. It must be the wine on top of the grass. Michael had had too much.

He closed his eyes.

Fourteen

He really didn't believe his brother.

Sam marched into the room. He had tried to get Michael up before, but this time it was on his mother's orders. That meant he could do just about anything to get his brother out of bed.

"Michael, come on!" Sam called. "It's after noon already!"

He yanked open the blinds.

Michael groaned, trying to shield his eyes from the light.

"Oh, shit!" he exclaimed after a second. "I was supposed to be at work at seven!"

"I tried to wake you up all morning, but you just growled."

Sam didn't add that he had been a little worried about him. Every time he had looked into the room, Michael had been tossing and turning violently, as if he were fighting with something. He seemed to be having a nightmare that lasted all morning.

Michael didn't make a move to get up. Sam hit his brother's foot with the back of his hand. "You can make it up to me by giving me a ride to the comic-book store."

Michael groaned again. "Go away!" He pulled the covers up over his head.

Sam sighed and left the room. His brother was hopeless.

Sam hoped Mom would understand his failure. She had gone to work, anyway. He wouldn't have to explain it to her until tonight.

In the meantime there was nothing to do. He went downstairs to find Nanook in the living room. The dog would understand.

He heard Grandpa working in the next room, the place where he kept all his stuffed animals. He had left the door open a little bit. Sam and Nanook wandered over to check it out.

They stopped in the doorway, trying to be as quiet as possible.

"All right," Grandpa said. He moved slightly away from his bench so that Sam could see what he was doing. "You make your first incision along the back and work the skin down both sides until reachin' the critter's legs. At this point you pull the skin down over the legs, inside out, until the toes are reached."

Sam turned around and left as quietly as he had come. He didn't particularly want to watch any more. Maybe there would be something to do out back. He and Nanook went out to the kitchen.

Sam glanced out the window at Grandpa's battered old pickup. He had hoped there might be something interesting that Grandpa had left in the back, some rope, maybe even an old tire so that Sam could make a swing.

His hopes were dashed as soon as he looked at the flatbed. There was nothing here but fenceposts. What could you do with fenceposts?

Nanook barked at his side. Maybe it was time to feed the dog.

"Nanook," he said, opening a can of Alpo, "this is my life. I come from a broken home. My mother works all day. My brother sleeps all day. And my Grandpa, who is possibly an alien, stuffs chipmunks."

That, he thought, pretty much summed up his situation. Nanook licked his hand in sympathy. But what to do next? He could, he supposed, walk into town. Right now, though, he didn't know if he had the energy. It would be a lot easier if his brother would get up and give him a ride. There was nothing to do in the house, and there didn't seem to be much more to do outside.

He stopped suddenly and looked back out the window. There, right above the sink, in easy reach, was Grandpa's marijuana bush. Michael had pointed out the bush to him yesterday, but he had forgotten all about it.

Sam walked over to the sink and reached through the open window. Well, why not? He knew both his mother and brother had smoked the stuff, and he guessed that Grandpa did too. It would certainly be something he'd never tried before. He walked over to the kitchen table to get some matches. Nanook barked excitedly at his heels.

He patted his dog's head to keep him quiet. Even though everybody else had done it, he wasn't too sure how the rest of his family would react to his experiment. Older people were like that sometimes. Sam wondered just how you did this. You smoked the stuff just like a cigarette, right? Well, maybe if you broke off a leaf and rolled it up, you could light that. Sam already had a leaf. He tore it in half and rolled that half as tight as he could.

"Whatcha doin?"

Oh, no! Sam hid the torn leaf in his hand and spun around.

"Grandpa, stop doin' the Indian Walk!"

The old man smiled and shrugged. "Gotta keep in practice. It's a dyin' art. Want to go into town with me?"

All right! That was more like it! Sam instantly agreed. Going into town was better than trying to smoke leaves any day.

Grandpa led him around the side of the house and into

the garage. Sam hadn't been inside the garage before. He had assumed, with the pickup parked outside, that the garage would be filled with junk. But it was quite neat inside, with a long workbench along one wall, and, next to the bench, a bright two-tone, blue-and-white 1957 Chevy.

Sam didn't know that much about cars, but his brother did, and Michael thought the 1957 Chevy was just about the neatest car ever invented. He used to build models of them in their basement back in Phoenix. That's why Sam recognized the car right off. It looked just like Michael's models, only bigger and in better shape.

Grandpa pulled down an old coffee can from the shelf above his workbench. He peered inside and pulled out a set of car keys.

"Get in!" he called to Sam. Sam climbed in the passenger seat as Grandpa slid behind the wheel.

Grandpa gingerly put the key into the ignition, then gently turned it. The engine caught instantly, then settled to a gentle purr.

"Got to let her warm up a bit," Grandpa explained. "Hear that, Sam? Just like a baby pussycat."

Sam didn't know if it sounded like a cat. He did know it sounded a lot better than Mom's old Land Rover. Boy, would Michael be jealous when he found out Sam got to ride in a '57 Chevy!

"Okay?" Grandpa revved the engine. "Let's go to town!" He reached forward and turned off the ignition.

What was going on here?

Grandpa climbed out of the car and put the keys back into the coffee can, and the can back on the top shelf.

He turned around and peered back into the car at Sam.

"Are we havin' fun or what?"

Sam stared back at his grandfather. "I thought we were going into town?"

Grandpa scratched his mustache. "That's about as close to town as I like to get."

He stood with a groan and wandered back out into the yard.

This was his grandfather's idea of fun? Sam knew it now. This was it. His life was definitely over.

Fifteen

Michael couldn't remember when he had felt this bad.

Even the light hurt his eyes today. He had to wear sunglasses just to see. He had managed to get downstairs by holding on to the railing, but now what? He had to get himself together. He wanted to go and see if he could work on the beach this afternoon. At this rate, he wasn't even going to make it out of the house.

He walked out to the back porch and saw his weights. That would do it! A good workout always made him feel better. He lifted his small barbells, taking one in each hand, and pumped them over his head. His arms shook. He tried to pump them again but couldn't get them above his shoulders. He knelt down and let the barbells drop to the floor. It was hopeless.

He walked back into the kitchen and sat heavily on one of the straight-backed chairs. Sam was in there, too, going through the refrigerator.

Sam paused in his exploration long enough to look back at his brother.

"What did *you* do last night?" Sam asked. "You look totally wasted."

Michael shook his head. "I can't remember much after the Chinese food that looked like maggots."

"Maggots?" Sam made a face and closed the refrigerator door. He walked over to Michael. "You don't suppose Grandpa's an alien, do you?"

Nanook followed. The dog began to lick Michael's feet.

"Beat it, Nanook!" Michael swiped halfheartedly at the dog. Nanook's tongue just felt too strange.

Sam pulled the dog away, then frowned and squatted to look at Michael's feet.

"Did you spill something?" he asked.

"No." Michael started to shake his head but stopped when he began to feel dizzy. "Why?"

"The bottoms of your feet are covered with salt," his brother replied.

This was just too much to deal with. Michael stood up with a groan and began to shuffle out of the room.

"I told you it was pretty weird Chinese food," Michael called to his brother as he walked out the door.

"Wanna go to the comic-book store?" his brother called back.

"No," was Michael's reply. Michael didn't want to do anything ever again.

If you want to do something right, you have to do it yourself. Sam was sure somebody famous had said that once, but he wasn't sure who. Maybe it was just his mother during one of her "Keeping your room clean" lectures.

But whoever said it, Sam knew he was going to have to live by it. If he was going to do anything in Santa Carla, the only one he would be able to depend on was himself.

He locked his bike to the stand and walked into the comic-book store. The Frog Brothers were in the back, stuffing comics into plastic bags. That was the one problem with this place. If you wanted to look at the comics, you also had to look at the Frog Brothers.

Edgar and Alan Frog glared back at Sam and stood up from where they had been working. Sam decided he'd just as soon not have another weird conversation with those two. His day had been weird enough already. He walked over to the first bin in the store. When the Frogs noticed how intent he was at looking at the books, maybe they'd leave him alone.

Edgar and Alan were walking toward the front of the store. Sam realized the bin he had picked was full of *Archie* comics. *Archie* comics? Oh, well, anything was better than talking to the Frogs.

Edgar came up next to him. "Don't read this crap, man. It promotes a dickhead mentality."

If he ignored them, Sam thought, maybe they would just go away. He did his best to study a cover of *Archie's TV Laugh-Out*.

Alan walked over to his other side. Apparently, ignoring them wasn't going to work.

"Noticed anything unusual about Santa Carla yet?" Alan asked.

Sam put his comic down. "Yeah. It's a pretty cool place if you're a Martian."

Edgar nodded solemnly. "Or a vampire."

Sam looked at the two brothers in disbelief.

"Are you guys sniffing old newsprint or something?"

The bell rang as the front door opened. All three of them glanced over to see a teenage girl and guy enter the store. But Sam knew that guy, even with the hat and sunglasses he was wearing. He was the Surf Nazi, the guy who had overturned Sam's fun tube.

Edgar punched Sam's arm to get his attention. "You think you're cool, don't you? You think you know what's really happening, don't you? Well, you don't know shit, buddy!"

What were they talking about? Didn't the brothers know this guy was the one who ripped them off the other night?

"Yeah," Alan added, "you think we just work in a comic-book store for our folks, huh?"

Sam had had just about enough of this. He looked up at the comic-filled rafters. "This isn't a comic-book store, right? It's a bakery."

"This is just our cover, man," Edgar insisted. "We're dedicated to a higher purpose. Truth, justice, and the American way."

The Surf Nazi was walking quickly around the store. Sam saw him stuff a comic book in his pants.

Then Edgar handed Sam a comic.

"Hey, man, get this," he insisted. "Only a buck."

Sam looked at the comic now in his hands. It was called *Destroy All Vampires*.

He tried to give it back. "I told you I don't like horror comics."

Neither Alan nor Edgar would take it.

"Think of this more as a survival manual," Alan added. "We put our number right on the back."

Sam turned the comic over. There was the phone number, written right under the price.

"And pray," Alan added, "that you never need to call us."

"I'm gonna pray that I never need to call you," Sam agreed.

The Surf Nazi and his girlfriend were heading for the door. The Frog Brothers got there before them.

"That'll be ten-eighty," Edgar said, palm out to accept the money.

"And five-seventy-five," Alan added, "for what you stole the other night."

The Surf Nazi stared at both of them for a long moment. Then he started to laugh. The bell rang furiously as the shop's door slammed open. It was the rest of the Surf Nazi gang. They gathered around their leader to stare down at the Frogs.

"Hey." The guy with the sunglasses sneered. "Call the cops."

"We have our own way of settling the score," Edgar added simply.

The Nazis laughed and made rude noises with their

tongues. The guy with the shaved head pushed Edgar and Alan back as the gang left. Sam could still hear them laughing as they all jumped into an old car and roared off down the street.

Sam wasn't so sure that the Surf Nazis should mock the Frogs quite so much. Edgar had talked about settling the score. Sam got the feeling that once the Frog Brothers got serious, they got *serious*. Sam knew that the Surf Nazis hadn't heard the end of this. And he also knew he didn't want to be around when they did.

Sam paid for his vampire comic and left. He'd had enough excitement for one day. It was time to go back to boring old Grandpa's house.

Sixteen

Her workday was over at last. Maria the cashier had been right. The closer it got to the weekend, the busier it got in the video store. When Lucy started work a couple of days ago, she had worried that there wouldn't be enough to do. Now she knew enough not to be worried; she had spent the entire day on her feet.

She got her purse and sweater from the closet, waved goodbye to Maria, and was out the door. It was a nice night, warm without being hot, with a bright starry sky overhead. It would be a pleasant night for a drive. Lucy took a deep breath. It was wonderful just to be outside.

Not that the job wasn't going well enough. She could hardly believe her luck in the way things had worked out so far in Santa Carla. Her father took right to the boys in his own particular way, and both Sam and Michael seemed to be making new friends. And then she practically had this video store job fall in her lap. Everything was going her way. It was another sign of her clear break with the past she'd left behind in Phoenix.

It was exciting, starting out fresh like this and making things work. She was sure that's why she had latched on to the first attractive man she had met in Santa Carla. The evening that Max had talked to her, and then hired her for the job, he had seemed so different and so dynamic compared to what she'd left behind in Phoenix. More than that, he had seemed as interested in her as she might be in him. She had just assumed something would happen between them. He was one more thing going right in Santa Carla.

She realized now that she had been mistaken; any thought of a relationship between the two of them had been pure wishful thinking. Max hadn't shown up once since she started working for him. He hadn't even bothered to call to ask how she was doing.

He was busy opening the new store. That seemed to be all that mattered to him. Maria told her that Max usually showed up an hour or two before the store closed to do a little financial business back in the office. Besides that, she never heard from him, either.

Oh, well, maybe this had all been a little too easy. Lucy would just have to go out and meet some other attractive, unattached men. There had to be at least one or two more in Santa Carla.

She had parked her car in the municipal lot down the street. Lucy fished for her keys as she walked. It always took her a minute to find her keys. Why did she always keep all this junk in her purse, anyway?

She heard the sound of motorcycles coming down the street. She looked up, half expecting to see Michael stopping by to say hello. Instead she saw the boys Michael had been talking to the other night. They slowed their bikes as they got close. Lucy smiled and waved to them. The boy in the lead grinned back. So they remembered her as well.

She stopped walking, waiting for the boys on the bikes to pass. They swung around her instead. She glanced behind her. The boy in the lead was still smiling. Were they playing some sort of joke on her?

The lead biker roared past her right side, then veered sharply left. Lucy was startled by how close his bike had come; she could have reached out and touched his leather jacket. The other three followed the first one's lead, swooping close to Lucy, then veering around behind her. Lucy couldn't move. They had her trapped in their circle of bikes.

Lucy looked around, searching for a way out. What did they want? They wouldn't do anything to her here. Would they? They were only a few feet away from Max's Video, in the middle of a city, for God's sake! Somebody could come out of a store or restaurant at any minute and see what was happening. But nobody did. The only people on the street were her and the bikers.

All of them were smiling at her now. She wondered exactly how friendly those smiles were. They were the same gang Max had thrown out of his store the other night. Why had they come back here? Did their parents know they did this sort of thing?

Lucy started walking. She was too old for this kind of prank. She wasn't going to be cowed by these teenagers. She'd get into her car or make it to one of the business establishments that was still open on the Boardwalk.

The leader of the bikers turned his cycle sharply and headed straight toward her. He gunned the engine.

Lucy stopped dead. He was going to hit her!

A pair of headlights swept around a corner up ahead and rapidly approached them. The car slowed as it came near, and Lucy realized that Max was behind the wheel of the red Corvette.

The Lost Boys shouted and laughed as they pulled away from Lucy. Still smiling, their leader nodded to Max, then the four of them roared off into the night. Max frowned as he watched them go.

Lucy realized that she had just found a white knight. Max parked in front of the store. She walked over to his car to thank him for scaring away the boys. Max turned back to her, his face full of concern.

"Playing their pranks again, huh?" he asked. Lucy nodded.

"I wouldn't worry about them," he said reassuringly. "They wouldn't hurt you."

Lucy looked after the bikes, their brake lights now fading in the distance. "Are you sure of that?"

Max grinned ruefully. "Oh, I know them all too well. That's one of the problems with running a video store in Santa Carla: You meet all the kids. Believe me, you're perfectly safe with that bunch."

Lucy repressed a shiver. Perfectly safe? She wasn't so sure Max knew them as well as he claimed. Still, she knew he was trying to reassure her, and she did feel better when she looked at his big, friendly face. Maybe she was overreacting to what had happened.

Max's dog sat in the Corvette's passenger seat. She reached over to pet his large golden head.

"Hi, Thorn," she said.

Thorn panted back at her.

She glanced up to see Max watching her.

"You know, Lucy," he said, "this isn't working out the way I had planned."

Lucy felt her heart stop for an instant. What did he mean by that? Was there something wrong with the way she was doing her job.

"I never get to see you," Max continued with a shrug. "Which is, of course, why I hired you in the first place."

He reached his hand out to gently brush against hers.

"How about dinner one night this week?"

So she wasn't wrong about Max, after all. He was just the sort of man who liked to take his own sweet time. Now that he had finally showed interest, though, she wasn't sure what she should say. What if a new relationship with Max turned out as badly as her marriage?

Lucy realized she was second-guessing herself again. She could spend the rest of her life thinking of the pros and cons of everything she did. It could take up her time nicely and keep her from ever doing anything at all.

She said yes, she'd love to.

Max asked her about tomorrow night. She said that was fine.

Why not? Things had their own way of working out, no matter what you thought.

Lucy glanced in her purse one more time as she walked away. The car keys were sitting right on top.

Interlude

So you want to know a little bit more about Santa Carla? Well, it's just about time to continue our tour. We've seen both the pier and the Boardwalk. Let's go a little farther out of town, to a promontory that overlooks the ocean.

If you come to this lookout most any evening, you'll find a car or two, and even more on weekends. There was only one car there this particular night, an old battered-up Ford. And its two occupants were doing what people usually did when they parked up on the lookout.

You've met the occupants, too, although you've never been introduced. One of them's name was Greg, but you'd know him as the leader of the Surf Nazis. You know, the one who liked to steal comic books. In fact, there were stolen comic books thrown all over the front seat of the Ford. Greg was in the back seat with his girlfriend, Shelly. You wouldn't be able to see inside the car, unfortunately; the windows had gotten all steamed up. You might say they were exercising. And they had been exercising for some time when Shelly pushed Greg away.

"What's the matter?" Greg managed to ask after he had disengaged himself from Shelly's sweater.

Shelly looked around the car. "I thought I heard something."

Greg laughed and started to kiss her again, his hands moving up and down her body. After a minute she couldn't help herself and replied in kind.

That's when the top of the car got ripped off. The whole

top of the car. And Shelly found Greg plucked from her arms and dragged straight up into the sky.

Shelly screamed. She tried to crawl over the back of the car, to somehow get away. It was useless, of course.

She was next.

Seventeen

The walls and ceiling of the cave seemed to be closing in on him.

He knew this was going to hurt. Michael shut his eyes tight. He wasn't so sure he should be doing this.

"Ouch!" he complained.

"Don't be a baby," Star replied. "That didn't hurt and you know it."

He moved his hand toward the ear she had just pierced. Star swatted it away. He looked at her reproachfully and saw that she was staring at his ear. She frowned and ran her tongue over the bottoms of her upper teeth. What was the matter? Could something have gone wrong?

Star picked up a wad of cotton and wiped a drop of blood away, then threaded a small gold hoop through the new hole.

"All right," Michael said, standing. Star had been right. It really hadn't been bad at all. He had thought he'd feel the loss of blood or something, but he wasn't even dizzy.

He gingerly touched the new hoop in his ear.

"Now the Lost Boys don't have anything on me."

Star didn't reply, instead busying herself cleaning up from her recent operation. Michael looked over to Laddie, who stood by the entrance to the cave, but the kid was watching the waves crashing to shore in the moonlight.

Star walked over to Michael when she was done. He took her hand.

"You know," he said, "I wouldn't have given my mom such a hard time about moving here if I'd known I was going to meet you."

Star grimaced at the mention of his mother. "I used to fight with my family—all the time," she began hesitantly. "Then I just got fed up and ran away. Now Laddie and the others are my family."

What did she mean, family? David and Star had seemed awfully close to each other from the first time he'd seen them together. Michael couldn't help it. He wanted Star for his own. He had to find out what the two of them really meant to each other.

He began slowly. It was his turn to hesitate.

"You and David . . . you seem very in tune with each other. That is, you seem very close—"

Star squeezed his hand. "I was just sleeping on the beach when David found me and brought me here. But we're not close like you mean." She paused again, as if searching for just the right words. "Besides, David and the boys have secrets—things they never tell me—things I don't want to know."

Michael took Star's other hand and looked into her eyes. He didn't want to talk about the Lost Boys and their secret gang rites. He wanted to talk about her.

"Does your family know you're okay?" he asked.

"I hope so," she replied. "I miss them sometimes really badly."

"Why don't you get in touch with them?"

"No." She shook her head with sad finality. "No, everything's different now."

He hated to see her look that sad. He promised himself that if there was anything he could do about it, he would keep her from ever getting sad again. He wanted to protect her from anything bad that had ever happened to her in the past, and anything else that might happen in the future.

Michael drew Star to him. They kissed.

He had never felt a kiss like that before. Her lips were so soft, so giving. Her touch made his whole body tingle. Her kiss warmed that electricity into a quiet fire. Nothing had ever felt this good before. Kissing her, Michael was truly alive.

They kissed again and again. He felt as if they were perfectly in tune, every kiss doubling their passion.

She kissed his neck. It sent shivers racing down his spine. He kissed her neck in turn, so white, so soft. He wanted to hold her as tight as he could, to taste her tongue against his again and again, to breathe in the faint, sweet odor of her skin, to hear her soft breathing and little moans of delight, to open his eyes and see her dark pupils only inches away. He wanted to be one with her.

Her teeth nipped at his neck, and it felt even better, the sweetest agony he had ever known. He kissed her forehead, and then his own mouth moved beneath her chin to her pure, pale neck.

Michael stopped. It had suddenly gotten dark. Someone stood in the middle of the room, blocking the light from the hurricane lantern.

He looked up to see David and Dwayne and Paul and Marco and Laddie, all five of them in a line, watching the two of them kiss.

David smiled. "Not interrupting anything, I hope."

Star backed out of their embrace.

"Look," she said. She pointed at Michael's pierced ear.

David nodded his approval. "You're almost one of us now, Michael."

Michael shook his head, trying to clear it. He could still taste Star on his lips and tongue, smell her in his nostrils, feel her with his whole body, from his fingertips to his toes. He found it difficult to think. Was he becoming a Lost Boy?

"Not really," he answered when he could find the words.

David laughed softly and waved for Michael to get up.

"Get your bike. We're going someplace."

Michael turned to Star, but she was watching David.

"Don't worry," David chided. "She'll be here when you get back."

Michael stood up. What should he do? There were still rules here that he didn't understand. He thought he had figured out one of the more obvious ones, though. It was fine for him to spend time with Star—in fact, they could do whatever they wanted—as long as he got along with the rest of the group. And sometimes "getting along" meant following David's orders.

Michael wanted to be with Star. He wanted it more than anything else he had ever wanted in his life. If he needed to go out on a run with the Lost Boys a couple of times in order to do that, it wasn't going to kill him.

Michael grinned at Star and Laddie a final time as he followed the Boys out of the cave. There was another reason, too, for going with David and the others. Despite all their jokes and attitude, Michael really felt they wanted him to be their friend.

They climbed over the moonlit rocks to get their bikes. The first time he had done this, Michael had been petrified. Now it got easier with every trip. It was just practice, he guessed. That, and how well his eyes had started to adjust to the moonlight. He hardly believed how well he could see. It was almost as bright as day.

Star stared out the cave entrance long after Michael had left with David and the others. They had left her behind with Laddie. And with her thoughts. She stared out at the ocean, going over and over what had happened.

For a while, when she first joined the Lost Boys, time seemed to stand still. There were no more worries about her parents, no more worries about anything in the outside world. David had introduced her to a fascinating new world. She looked on him almost as a magician, except that all his tricks seemed to be real.

But that all changed when she met Michael. Now the

world was going much, much too fast. She had known what David wanted Michael for from the very beginning. She had wanted to warn Michael away, but she just couldn't. There had been something about him from the first, the way he had approached her, shy and forward all at the same instant. For the first time since she could remember, Star saw someone that she might really care about.

She had been so relieved at first, when David had accepted Michael as Star's friend and brought him into the Lost Boys. It was only later that she realized what would have to happen if he was going to stay. If only she could get him alone for long enough and get up the courage to really talk to him.

But how could she? She was sure he would leave if she told him the truth. And she wanted him too much to give him up.

Michael had come here of his own free will. He had made his choice. They all had made their choices. Now Michael was going to be one of them, whether he knew it or not.

"Star?" Laddie looked up at her, his eyes worried below his ragged bangs. He was so young. Why did he have to be here too?

Star asked him what was wrong.

"I had the dream again," he said softly, almost in a whisper, "about *them*."

"Who, Laddie?"

Laddie paused before he spoke, as if trying to remember everything in his dream. He began slowly. "The big guy in the yard, hammering something . . . and the woman with the red hair. I was there too—and, and a dog! We were all laughing." He looked up at her, confused and afraid.

"Laddie," She hugged the boy tight against her. "You can still remember. You can still remember home!"

The boy shook his head. "It was a dream, Star."

Star shook her head back at him. "No, Laddie. It was a memory."

They heard the sound of bikes starting up in the distance.

"You didn't tell David?" Star asked.

"No," Laddie replied softly.

"Promise me you'll keep it that way." She grabbed the boy's shoulders and looked into his eyes. "You're not like the others, Laddie. You're like me."

She paused to swallow. Her throat was very dry. She thought of dreams she had had, of her mother and sister, her bedroom overlooking the garage. She couldn't remember the little things about her house as clearly as she once did, couldn't quite see their faces with the clarity of day-to-day life. When she saw them now, it was as if she were looking through a haze, or a TV picture full of snow. But she still saw them in dreams.

She told the boy, "I can still remember too."

She hugged Laddie to her again as she heard the motorcycles roar off down the beach.

"You like Michael," Laddie stated after a moment.

"I like Michael," Star agreed.

Laddie looked up at her again, his eyes still full of worry.

"You better not like him too much."

She nodded and kept on hugging Laddie, mostly, she realized, to keep herself from crying. Maybe nothing would happen. Maybe she and Michael could leave and start a new life.

But she knew in her heart that Laddie was right. Maybe it would be better if she just went back to sleep. Maybe then she could dream of someplace she could call home.

Eighteen

It was almost impossible to see. A night fog had come up from the ocean and blanketed the hills above the beach in gray. Michael could barely make out the red taillights of the motorcycles in front of him on the road.

It must be well after midnight by now, late enough so they weren't meeting any other traffic. Still, he was amazed at how fast they were all going through the middle of the fog. David was in the lead as usual, and he never slowed down until he got where he wanted to be.

David pulled to a stop up ahead. Michael and the other Lost Boys joined him. They had stopped by the edge of a bridge of some sort. Michael got off his bike to join the others, who stood on the edge of the embankment, where the bridge began. As Michael approached them he saw a pair of glistening rails close by David's boots. The bridge must be a railroad trestle.

Michael saw David nod appreciatively at the fog.

"Perfect time," was all their leader said. He walked out onto the trestle.

"What's going on?" Michael asked.

David smiled at that. He looked back to the next Lost Boy in line.

"What's going on, Marco?"

"I dunno." Marco shrugged and turned to the next Lost Boy. "What's goin' on, Paul?"

"Who wants to know?" Paul asked.

"Michael wants to know," David replied, his voice full of mock seriousness. The Lost Boys all laughed.

So they were going to make a joke of it again. Michael knew it was another one of David's tests. David was looking for an easy way to get Michael's goat, a way to get him mad and exclude him from the Lost Boys. Maybe even a way to keep him away from Star. Michael could take anything David could dish out.

The Lost Boys walked out onto the railroad trestle. Michael followed. Thick railroad ties, spaced a couple of feet apart, supported the track to either side. Michael stepped carefully from one tie to the next. There was nothing between the ties at all but air. The trestle seemed to cross a deep gorge. Michael hated to think what would happen if one of them slipped and fell. There was no way to tell how far below the chasm reached. The fog closed in again about twenty feet below.

Marco, Paul, and Dwayne were in the lead, well out onto the trestle by now. Then Marco disappeared. Michael stared through the fog, trying to make out what was going on. Paul and Dwayne dropped between the ties; they just stepped out into the air and fell. What were they doing? David didn't seem to react one way or the other. Michael knew it was hopeless to ask.

David looked back at him.

"Now you, Michael."

With that thought Michael knew what David was doing now. This was another one of his tricks, like riding his bike through the flames, something that looked deadly but was nothing more than a simple stunt.

"Do it, Michael," David ordered. "Now!"

Well, if that's the way David wanted it, it was all right with Michael. Michael sat down on one railroad tie and grabbed onto the next. He saw David climb down a few ties away. Then Michael swung down below the trestle.

David's body dropped down a moment later. David had positioned himself to face Michael. The leader of the Lost Boys grinned.

So, Michael thought, he had passed another test. He wondered just how far the drop was from here. Then he felt the railroad tie vibrate in his hands.

For a second he thought it might be an earthquake. Then he heard the whistle blow, and the rumble of iron wheels.

A train was coming.

"Hang on!" David called over the deafening noise.

The vibration doubled with every second. Michael could feel his sweating hands slipping on the wood. He had been wrong. They didn't have to just hang from the trestle. They had to manage not to lose their grip while a train roared overhead.

Michael realized that the test had just begun.

The train was above them with a scream of air and a thunder of wheels. They were surrounded by smoke and heat and dust. Michael tried to strengthen his grip, but the vibration was slowly pulling his fingers loose. He looked at the others through watery eyes. He was sure they'd all done this before. They probably knew a secret to help keep from falling.

And then he saw Paul fall and disappear into the fog. Michael wasn't sure if he slipped or if he let go. He tried to listen for a scream, or the sound of Paul's body hitting something, but all he could hear was the roar of the train.

Then Marco fell. A moment later Dwayne let go and vanished below.

He realized David was screaming something at him, over and over.

"Let go, Michael!" he was saying. "Let go!"

Michael looked down at his feet. How far was the drop in the fog?

"Do it!" David exhorted. "Be one of us!"

That was it. David was telling Michael this was another one of their tricks. The fall couldn't be very far at all. Why else would the other three Lost Boys have already gone?

One of Michael's hands slipped free of the wood. He dug the nails of his remaining hand into the wood overhead, his body swinging back and forth over the void.

"Do it, Michael!" David called. "I gave you Star, didn't I?"

Then David let go and dropped into the fog.

The final car of the train passed overhead. The noise and vibration began to fade. Michael swung the hand that had slipped back up to reestablish his grip.

He heard laughter down below.

"Do it, Michael!" one voice called. "Let's go!" another added. They whistled and shouted. "It's safe! Come on!"

You only live once. Michael took a deep breath and let go.

He didn't fall. Not really. He felt, rather, as if he were floating, buoyed up by the ocean breeze, weightless in the middle air. Michael laughed.

And he fell. With a horrible suddenness, the wind screaming in his ears. He was falling forever. He felt as if he were blacking out.

He opened his eyes and realized that David was holding Michael in his arms. The Lost Boy grinned down at him.

"Almost," David said.

"Michael! Wake up! It's Mom!"

Sam's voice cut through his dreams. Dreams of falling into a hole that opened beneath him in the earth, a hole that would swallow him up and leave him trapped. He looked around at the rich brown earth as he fell and saw that it was moving, alive with slithering, dark worms and crawling maggots that were the color of the moon.

Someone was shaking his shoulder. Michael opened his eyes.

His brother looked down at him.

"Mom's home?" Michael mumbled.

"No," Sam replied. "On the phone."

Michael groaned and turned so that he could see his alarm clock. It was two o'clock in the afternoon!

"Oh, shit," Michael moaned. "Mr. Walker down at the beach will never hire me again."

Michael sat up. The light in here hurt his eyes. The shades were drawn, but the afternoon sun beat through the cracks. It was still too bright in here. He fumbled on the night table until he found his sunglasses.

"Oh, cool, *mon*!" Sam remarked as Michael slipped the glasses on. "Beyond Don Johnson!"

Michael tried to think of a suitable reply but decided to forget it. When you felt as bad as he did, things like little brothers were better left ignored.

But Sam wasn't done yet. "Michael," he asked with a wiggle of his eyebrows, "are you freebasing? Inquiring minds want to know!"

Michael glared at Sam and picked up the phone.

"Hi, Mom."

"Michael," his mother's voice replied, "are you still in bed?"

"No," he lied. "I'm up."

His mother seemed to accept it. "Michael, will you do me a favor this evening? Will you stay home with Sam tonight? I'm meeting Max for dinner after work."

What? She wanted him to waste his evening with that little creep of a brother?

"Can't Grandpa watch him?" he asked.

"Grandpa has plans of his own."

"So do I! Sam's old enough to stay alone."

"Michael." His mother's voice turned suddenly cold. "You've been coming home in the middle of the night. You sleep all day. Sam is *always* alone." Her voice softened again. "Come on, be a pal."

Michael recognized that icy tone of voice. Once Mom got that way, you either gave in or got into real trouble.

"Okay?" his mother prompted.

"Okay," Michael agreed at last. Satisfied, his mother said good-bye.

He looked at his hand as he put down the phone. Wow, were his fingernails getting long! He'd have to cut them. He wondered why they were growing so fast. It probably had something to do with the sea air.

"You have a rough life," Sam quipped. "Money for nothing and your chicks for free."

Michael suppressed another groan as he got out of bed. You could take Sam away from MTV, but you couldn't get MTV out of Sam. He walked silently around his brother. He might have to spend time around Sam, but nobody said anything about having to talk to him.

He slammed the bathroom door behind him and pulled off his underpants, then turned on the shower. A little hot water would get him going. He turned on both of the faucets.

The water came on with a whoosh. He gave it a couple seconds for the hot water to start up, then stuck his arm in to test the temperature. Michael almost cried out in pain. The water was much too hot. He quickly reached over and turned down the hot-water faucet. Too hot, too hot!

He realized that he had turned the hot water off. It didn't make any difference. The water still burned. He pulled his arm from the shower.

What was the matter with the shower? He looked at the angry red welts running down his arm.

The cold water had burned him.

Nineteen

This was living. There was nothing in the world like a good bologna sandwich. Unless, of course, you had a Twinkie or two to go with it. Unfortunately Sam had determined that there wasn't a Twinkie in the house. To make up for it he had made two bologna sandwiches.

Grandpa wandered into the kitchen. To Sam's amazement he was wearing a coat and tie.

Grandpa opened a cupboard over Sam's head, peered inside, and frowned. He looked down at Sam.

"Anything in here that might pass for after-shave?"

Sam thought for a second. There might be something under the sink. He opened the doors and studied the under-sink contents critically until he finally found something that at least was the right color. He passed the bottle to his grandfather.

Grandpa looked at the bottle of Windex Sam had given him with some skepticism, then squirted a little bit of it into his palm. He sniffed it, nodded, and splashed it on his cheeks.

"Thanks." He handed the bottle back to Sam.

Michael staggered into the room. He looked terrible, like he hadn't slept in a week. Sam could tell from his expression that Grandpa noticed it, too, although the old man, like usual, didn't say anything about it. Grandpa, Sam knew by now, was a big believer in minding your own business.

"Big date, Grandpa?" Michael managed.

"Just dropping off some of my handiwork to the Widow Johnson." Grandpa stroked his mustache meaningfully.

"Oh, yeah?" Michael replied nastily. "What'd you stuff for her? *Mr.* Johnson?"

Grandpa picked up a squirrel that was almost as ugly as the woodchuck he'd given Sam. He glanced sternly at Michael for the briefest of moments, then walked out the door.

"See you later, boys."

Sam punched his brother's arm. "That wasn't funny, Michael."

Grandpa climbed into his pickup truck. He tooted his horn as he pulled out of the driveway. The horn played "La Cucaracha." Michael looked away for an instant as Grandpa turned on his headlights. Then Grandpa drove the pickup truck down the road, out of sight.

Michael just stood there, staring out the door.

"You gotta eat something for dinner," Sam said. "I'll make you a sandwich."

"Don't bother," Michael muttered.

Boy, Sam sure was glad that Michael decided to stay home with him. He always wanted to spend an evening with a zombie. Maybe there was some way he could cheer his brother up, to get him out of his funk. His brother needed a little good old-fashioned needling.

He stared at Michael's ear. "Lose the earring, Michael. It's not happening. It's just not happening."

"Piss off," Michael replied halfheartedly.

Sam shook his head. "All you do is give attitude lately. What's the matter? Have you been watching too much *Dynasty*?"

Michael didn't reply. Sam decided to sit down and eat. So his brother looked and sounded like a refugee from *Night of the Living Dead*. That was no reason to waste some perfectly good bologna.

Bright light flashed through the kitchen window and swept

across the room. Sam looked up from his sandwich. Headlights, maybe? Was Grandpa coming back?

Were they even headlights? They were almost too bright.

"What's that?" Michael asked, suddenly alert.

The lights were moving toward the other side of the house. Michael walked into the living room. Sam put down his sandwich and followed.

There was something going on outside. It sounded like somebody was whispering, although the whispering had to be really loud to come from the other side of the front door. Michael was standing in the middle of the room, hypnotized by the sound. Sam walked up next to his brother. Something was very wrong here.

The headlight glare swept across the living room curtains. This time, though, there was noise, too; the roar of motorcycles, as if the bikes were circling the house. Then there was a wind, a strong, cold wind, blowing back the curtains, rattling the pots and pans in the kitchen.

The whispering got louder, louder even than the wind, and Sam could make out the words.

"Michael," the whispering said. "Michael. Michael."

Michael walked toward the front door.

Sam ran after him. The whispering wasn't natural. This was all wrong.

"Don't open it!"

The engine roar increased. Whatever waited for them sat in their front yard, revving their bikes, ready for Michael to open the door.

Michael reached for the doorknob.

"No!" Sam screamed.

Michael opened the door, anyway, throwing it ajar.

Sam cautiously peered around his brother's side.

There was nothing there. The front yard was empty.

A blast of frigid air rushed into the house, like a wind from the dead of winter. There was a sound somewhere overhead, like night birds calling to each other far up in the sky. The wind rushed away, bending the distant trees as it escaped the yard.

Then everything was silent and still. Wisps of fog seemed to be gathering at the edge of the woods, crawling along just a few inches above the ground.

"Weird," Sam remarked.

Michael was alone at last. Sam had finally gone off to take a bath. Nanook had gone with him. That meant Michael had the whole first floor all to himself. It was what he'd wanted all night, just to be left alone.

There was something happening here. "Weird," his brother had said. For a change Sam had hit things right on the nose. It was weirder than weird.

And Michael had gotten himself right into the middle of it. It had something to do with Santa Carla, and the Lost Boys, maybe even with Star. Michael had changed since he had come here. And things outside his life were changing too. Michael felt as if everything were going crazy. Life was beyond his control.

No. There had to be a way to think things through, to figure out just what was happening here. He wouldn't let the Lost Boys get the better of him, no matter how lousy he felt. And somehow, he felt with a sudden certainty, he would get Star to leave them.

He could hear Sam's radio blasting all the way down here. Sam liked to sit in the bathtub and listen to the radio for half an hour at a time. Michael decided it might be a little quieter in the kitchen. Besides, his brother was right. He should put something in his stomach.

He opened the refrigerator and took out a carton of milk.

Pain shot through his stomach and chest. He doubled over, dropping the milk.

It was over as soon as it had begun. Michael opened his eyes and cautiously took a breath. It had felt for a moment like someone had taken a knife to his insides. And now, nothing.

He stood up from the squat he had fallen into when the pain hit. God, what had that been? He might be in more trouble than he thought.

He looked down and saw that the milk carton had burst where it had hit the floor. There was milk everywhere. He went to get the mop to clean it up.

He found the mop in the corner behind the refrigerator. He grabbed the smooth wooden handle, ready to carry it back to the spill.

The pain hit again, worse than before. Michael fell to his knees and clutched his stomach. It didn't do any good. His guts were being ripped out from the inside.

He lifted his head, trying to find some way to take his mind from the pain.

The walls of the kitchen were moving! They seemed to breathe, in and out, in and out. The cans and jars were doing the same. A soup can puffed toward him. Raspberry preserves crawled and wriggled behind the glass. The light bulb swelled, about to explode. The floor rippled and heaved beneath his knees.

Michael could feel his heartbeat. It was heavy inside his chest. His heart racked his whole body with its pulse, as if it wanted to break free of his rib cage and go bouncing across the pantry floor. He could feel the blood surge through his arteries and veins, pushing against the skin of his arms, his legs, his chest, his temples. He felt as if he might burst in a dozen places, great fountains of blood pouring from a dozen wounds.

Michael forced his head back down. He had to stop this somehow.

He saw a mouse in the corner. A large mouse in a trap, its neck slashed and broken, but not quite dead. It struggled feebly in the corner. And it bled. Bright red droplets fell to the kitchen floor.

The mouse pulsed and expanded, just like everything else around Michael. He didn't care. All he could see was the blood. The mouse stiffened, eyes wide open, dead at last. Michael dragged himself over toward the dead rodent, heedless of the pain in his stomach and chest.

He reached out his fingers to the pantry floor.

He had to touch the blood.

Twenty

Her stomach was all in knots. She had the urge for a cigarette for the first time in a year and a half. She was too old for this sort of thing.

How long had it been, Lucy wondered, since she had been on a date? And a first date, at that?

She and Lance had gotten married right out of college. It had been the thing to do back then, get married right away. People hadn't adjusted back then to couples just "living together." Plus there was always that grand and glorious specter of Vietnam. You might as well do what you can today, whether it was to get married or drop LSD, because tomorrow the guys would get drafted and next month they'd be dead.

It was a different world now. And Lucy was out in it, entirely on her own.

Enough philosophizing, she told herself. Get into the restaurant!

She walked through the front door of the Sea Cloud.

Max was waiting just inside. He smiled his roguish grin as she entered the room and plucked a rose from a bouquet on a table against the wall. He presented the flower to her with a flourish. Lucy accepted and decided Max got at least a couple points for style.

The main room of the restaurant was a bit too dark, almost too intimate. The maître d' led them to a corner table with a window view of the ocean, far away from the noise and bustle of the other diners. Lucy wouldn't be surprised if Max had planned that too. The maître d' left them each with a menu. She had to squint to read it in the room's half light. Still, she noticed right away that her menu didn't have any prices on it.

Max put down his menu. The waiter was there instantly.

"Ready to order now, sir?"

Lucy closed her menu and looked at Max.

"I'll just have the filet of sole."

"No you won't," Max replied. He glanced at the waiter. "We'll start with caviar. Caesar salad and your two biggest lobsters. And, I think, champagne." He flipped open the wine list for the briefest of moments. "Dom Perignon. Seventy-one."

"Very good, sir," the waiter replied, taking the menus and departing.

Max turned back to Lucy and frowned.

"Not impressed, huh?"

Lucy was flustered for an instant, surprised that her disappointment was so apparent. How could she explain it to him?

"Oh, I would have been" she said at last. "One marriage ago."

Max grinned. "So, I've met the one woman who's going to hold my success against me."

Lucy sighed. She had so wanted this evening to go right. It seemed now like it was headed in completely the wrong direction.

"You seem like a terrific person, Max," she said in an attempt to salvage something. "And I'm grateful for the job."

"But it's not really what you want to do, is it?" Max asked gently.

Lucy leaned across the table, intent on being understood. "I want to do anything that makes dragging Michael and Sam here to Santa Carla, against their will, easier on them."

Max leaned closer too. "You're a nurturer, Lucy, a

protector.'' He lowered his voice so that it was almost a growl. ''A lioness with her cubs.''

Lucy laughed despite herself. ''My cubs can't wait to get away from this lioness. I think my mothering days are nearly over.''

Max took her hand.

''They don't have to be,'' he said.

He needed more.

The mouse had helped. The pain was gone. But he knew it wouldn't last for long. He needed more.

He was calmer now. So calm. He needed to stay calm, away from the pain.

Rock music drifted down from the second floor. He climbed the stairs. The music grew louder, and so did the sound of his heart. His heart beat in time with the music as his feet glided up the stairs. His heartbeat grew stronger still. He reached the landing. He could barely hear the music coming from behind the closed bathroom door.

He walked toward the bathroom. His heartbeat was so loud. There was nothing but his heartbeat.

He stood outside the bathroom door.

He knew what his heart needed.

Sam sang along with the tape on his boom box. Clarence ''Frogman'' Henry croaked ''I Ain't Got No Home.'' Sam croaked along. He might not have a home, but this bathtub was the next best thing.

He had spent the last ten minutes with shampoo in his hair, sculpting it as he glanced appreciatively at the full-length mirror across from the tub. The punk styles he got were ten times better than anything the Surf Nazis ever even dreamed of. Sam had to admit it, he was one cool dude. Nanook sat by the side of the tub, watching everything Sam did with fascination. Occasionally the dog barked approval.

It was great, sitting here in the bathtub, radio up loud, especially when Mom wasn't around to tell him to turn the music down or to get out of the tub before he turned into a raisin.

Nanook stood up, sniffing. The dog walked to the door, whining softly.

What was the matter with Nanook? The dog didn't say. Sam went back to sculpting his hair.

Nanook whined again. Maybe the dog didn't like the song on the tape.

He stood outside the bathroom door. He could hear nothing but his heartbeat. He didn't want the pain to come again. He knew what he needed. So close, just the other side of this door. He reached for the knob.

And thought about his brother.

He pulled his hand away.

No! Sam was in there! Not Sam!

His heart pounded in his ears, drowning out everything else.

He put his back to the door, trying to fight what grew inside him.

His hand reached for the doorknob.

He knew what he needed.

Nanook was really getting restless.

Maybe, Sam thought, *I've spent enough time in the tub.* Who knows, maybe the dog had to go to the bathroom or something. He hated to think how mad his mom would get if the dog peed all over the carpet. He'd get out of the tub as soon as this song was over.

The dog made another noise deep in its throat.

Okay. Okay. Time to rinse the hair. Sam held his breath and dunked his head under the water.

He knew what he needed.

The door was locked. He smashed at the knob with the side of his fist. He didn't want the pain to come again. The door swung open, hard.

He was in the room.

The dog. He had forgotten about the dog.

The dog growled and leapt for him, pushing him into the hallway. The door slammed shut behind them.

What was that?

Sam had never heard such a racket before. It started just as soon as he had come up for air. Crashing and banging, growling and barking, it sounded like the villagers were fighting the Wolfman on the other side of the bathroom door.

There was another bumping sound. The villagers and the Wolfman seemed to have rolled down the stairs.

Then it was quiet.

Sam got out of the tub and wrapped a towel around his middle. What was going on out there? Michael must have had a real accident.

Then he realized that Nanook was gone. How had the dog gotten through the locked door?

He reached for the door and found that the lock was broken. The door swung open silently.

It was dark in the hall, but there was nobody there. Sam walked slowly down the stairs.

"Michael?" he called. "Are you there, Nanook?"

There was no reply. Sam swallowed and moved on down the stairs.

He stopped. He heard someone, or something, breathing heavily at the bottom of the stairs.

"Michael?" he asked.

"Don't turn on the light," his brother replied hoarsely.

What kind of trick was Michael trying to pull now? Sam turned on the light and screamed. His brother was huddled at the bottom of the stairs, his face and hands covered with blood.

"What happened, Michael?"

"Nanook . . ." His brother moaned.

Sam looked around. He didn't see the dog anywhere.

"What about Nanook?" he demanded. "What have you done to Nanook?" Sam was getting angrier with every word he shouted. "What have you done to my dog, you asshole?"

"Nothing!" Michael responded a bit louder than before. "I didn't hurt him. He bit me! This is *my* blood!"

Michael lifted his hand so that Sam could see the gash across his palm, a long, red, ugly thing. Sam took a step away. He heard Nanook's dog tags jingle across the front room. The dog appeared out of the darkness to sit next to him. What would make Nanook do something like that to Michael?

"What did you do to him, Michael?" Sam asked. "Why did he bite you?"

"He was protecting *you*!" Michael retorted.

Protecting me? Sam thought. His brother didn't make any sense. Protecting me from what?

Then Sam looked in the mirror. He realized, when he looked back at his brother, that his mouth was open.

"What?" his brother demanded.

Sam pointed. "Look at your reflection in the mirror!"

Michael looked and saw the same thing Sam had. Michael had almost no reflection at all. He looked like a ghost in one of those old movies, only faintly there. You could see the wall behind him, right through his body.

Oh, shit. Sam knew what it meant when you had no reflection.

"You're a creature of the night, Michael!" Sam turned his accusing finger on his brother. What had Michael gotten himself into this time? Sam saw that his hand was shaking. "Just like the comic book! You're a vampire,

Michael! My own brother, a goddamn, shit-sucking vampire!'' He swallowed. ''Just wait till Mom finds out!''

His brother stood up. Sam doubted that Michael believed him. The way he looked, Sam doubted that Michael knew what planet he was on.

Michael staggered toward the staircase.

''Stay away!'' Sam yelled. He made a cross with his index fingers and ran quickly up the stairs. Nanook was right behind him. Once inside his room, he slammed the door closed and locked it, then did the same with the door that led from his room to the bathroom.

Michael had already broken the lock on the other door. Neither of these locks were any stronger. Sam knew he didn't have much time.

He quickly found the vampire comic in the plastic bag. The Frogs' number was on the back.

He heard Michael, outside, climbing the stairs.

Twenty-one

Sam explained the situation as quickly as possible.

"You did the right thing, calling us," Edgar said on the other end of the phone. "Does your brother sleep a lot?"

"All day," Sam answered.

"Can't stand light?" It was Alan's voice this time.

"Wears sunglasses in the *house*," Sam agreed.

"Bad breath?" Edgar asked. "Long fingernails?"

Sam had to think about this one. "His fingernails are definitely longer," he said after a moment, "but he always had bad breath."

"Salt sticks to the bottom of his feet," Alan added.

"Yeah," Sam said. He'd almost forgotten about that.

"He's a vampire, all right," Alan said with finality.

"Get yourself a good sharp stake," Edgar advised, "and drive it through his heart."

"I can't do that!" Sam exclaimed. "He's my brother!"

"Okay," Alan replied reassuringly. "We'll come over and do it."

"No!" Sam cried.

"Well," Edgar advised, "you better get yourself a garlic T-shirt, buddy, or it's your funeral."

Sam hung up. This was worse than he thought.

What could he do?

Maybe if he could just go to sleep, everything would get better. Maybe it could all turn out to be a dream.

Michael flopped down on his bed, exhausted. He closed his eyes and could feel himself drifting. His muscles were so tired that he could barely feel the bed beneath him. He felt as if he were floating, so full of fatigue that he couldn't even fall asleep.

Something cold pressed against his nose. He opened his eyes. A long, white surface of some sort stretched before him. Was he dreaming at last? He blinked his eyes. It didn't feel like a dream. Where was he?

He looked around to see his bed, six feet below. That white space above him was the ceiling. He was floating.

Michael's heart wanted to stop beating. But this was impossible! How could he be weightless? His fright gave way to a cold determination. He was not going to let this happen. He still had some control over his life! He was going to turn himself around and get back down onto the bed.

He used his hands to push himself along the ceiling toward the window. Then, all he had to do was twist himself around and lower himself down with the blind cord. He pushed himself away from the ceiling and wall, trying to spin himself around so that he was facing downward.

There! He reached out his hand and grabbed the cord. But his body kept on spinning. His feet were moving in front of him now, straight toward the open window. Panic-stricken, Michael almost lost his grip on the cord. His fingertips brushed the windowsill as they passed.

Then he was outside the house, floating away on the wind.

What was he going to do? Sam couldn't kill his brother, no matter what the Frogs said. But what if Michael tried to kill him? Where were Mom and Grandpa when he really needed them?

The phone rang. Sam jumped up and grabbed it.

"Hello!" he shrieked into the receiver.

"Sam?" It was his mother's voice on the phone. His mother! "Is everything all right?"

"Mom," Sam replied, trying to calm his voice. "I think we've got to have a long talk about something."

"What's wrong?" his mother demanded. "Tell me."

What could he say to her? That Michael had turned into a vampire? She'd only believe it when she saw it herself.

"We can't talk about it on the phone," he answered. How could he get her to come home? Couldn't she hear how important it was?

There was something moving outside the window. Sam looked up. It was Michael, floating toward him.

"Oh, no!" Sam yelled. "Oh, God! He's coming to get me! Mom!"

He heard the phone drop at his mother's end.

Michael was coming right for him! Sam backed away. If his brother could fly, no place was safe.

Glass burst into the room as Michael's foot crashed through the bedroom window.

"Help me, Sam!" his brother screamed. "Help me!"

Sam looked back at Michael, who flailed in the air, halfway in the room, halfway over the back yard. His brother didn't look much like a vampire out there. In fact, his brother looked totally out of control.

Sam decided to help him.

"Stay there, Michael!" he called. "I'll get you!"

But the wind was back, a winter gale blowing through the window, so strong that it almost pushed Sam the other way. He fought against it, moving across the room with deliberate steps.

He grabbed Michael's foot.

The wind was gone. Sam began to pull his brother inside. Michael had no weight at all. It was like pulling a balloon.

He dragged his brother's head and shoulders into the room. Michael stared wide-eyed at Sam. He looked even more scared than Sam felt.

"We've got to stick together, Sam." Michael's voice shook as he spoke. "You've got to help me."

"What about Mom?" Sam asked as he quickly hauled him in.

"Please, Sam." If it was possible, Michael turned even paler. "Don't tell her."

"I don't know, Michael." Sam grabbed his brother's belt. "This is not like breaking a lamp or getting a *D*." He pulled on his brother's knees and then his shoes. Now all he had to figure out was a way to get Michael back on the ground.

"Just for a few days, Sam," Michael pleaded. "Give me a chance to work this out myself."

Yeah, Sam thought, if he could learn how to use gravity again. But Michael seemed more like his old brother with every passing moment. Maybe he was right, after all, and there was still some way Michael could work this out.

It was certainly easier than driving a stake through his heart.

Something was wrong at home. Really wrong. Lucy ran straight out to the Land Rover. She'd have to explain it all to Max later. She just hoped he would understand.

Luckily the restaurant was on the right side of town, only a few minutes drive away from their house. Her father's place was secluded, a bit off the main highways. Could there have been a burglar? Maybe she should have called the police.

But she hadn't had any time to call the police, or explain things to Max. She'd only had time to react, to jump in her car and drive twenty miles above the speed limit for home.

She jammed on the brakes as the Land Rover rushed into Grandpa's driveway. She was out of the car as soon as she could throw it into park, running for the house. The front door was unlocked. She rushed into the front hallway.

Sam ambled down the stairs in her direction.

"Sam!" she demanded. "Are you all right? You had me scared to death!"

Her son smiled apologetically. "Sorry, Mom. I thought I saw something out the window. I was reading a horror comic book, and I guess I got carried away."

What? That was all it was, after— And she had run out on the first date she had had since— Lucy looked sternly at her son, reminding herself that one should not murder one's own children.

"You know," she said all too slowly, "I've just about had it with the both of you. . . ."

She stalked past the stairs. She had never even gotten her dinner! Maybe she could find something in the kitchen that would calm her down.

"What happened in here?"

She couldn't believe it. You'd think her two boys would be old enough to take care of themselves. What a mess!

She heard Sam clomp down the stairs and walk in the kitchen behind her. She put her hands on her hips and surveyed the damage. A milk carton had smashed; there was milk all over the floor. The pantry was a mess too. Somebody had knocked over a mop. Who knows, maybe somebody had even intended to use it to clean up the spill, although they had obviously gotten sidetracked before they bothered to do any work. There were a couple cans and an old, bent mousetrap in the middle of the floor as well. Kids!

"You know," she said with a sigh, "I'd like to have a personal life too. It's just not fair."

She bent down and picked up the crumpled milk carton from the floor. She looked up at Sam.

"Where's Michael?"

Sam shrugged. "He went to bed early."

She put down the carton. Michael went to bed early? And Sam wasn't about to confess to this mess, either. Lucy wondered just who was responsible for the craziness around here. Nanook?

Interlude

Let me show you something else. Still in Santa Carla, but a little bit out of the way, even farther from the main roads than Grandpa's place. It's a nice, big ranch-style house with lots of land. It belongs to Max. Didn't know there was that much money in videotapes, did you? Well, believe me, Santa Carla is full of surprises.

On a quiet night like that, anything can happen.

Max got out of his car slowly. You could tell from the way he walked that he wasn't in the best of moods. Probably had something to do with his dinner with Lucy, or rather his nondinner. How could a woman just disappear like that? Of course, Lucy had called him at the restaurant with an explanation, but the call had come half an hour after she had left, and her excuse probably didn't make any sense.

You could tell from Max's attitude that it was just one of those nights.

Max stopped and listened. He had heard a noise. He walked cautiously toward his front porch. There it was again!

"Who's there?" he asked. There was no answer. He thought he heard something, though. Whispering? Giggling, maybe.

Then the great black shape swooped down on him. Max yelled, beating at the thing with his fists.

Wait a minute. Max grabbed the thing that had attacked him. It was a kite, a black plastic kite in the shape of a bat.

Motorcycles started up across the yard, headlights glaring. The bikes and their riders swept away from Max's yard, the roar of engines mixing with their laughter. An instant later Max was all alone.

It was only a practical joke, then? Max looked at the kite he still held in his hands.

This time it was only a joke.

Twenty-two

Shit!

Michael ducked out of sight as Grandpa pulled his pickup truck into the driveway. Michael had almost gotten caught in the headlights. He hid, back pressed against the side of the garage, waiting for the old man to go inside. He didn't want anybody to know he had left. He had things to find out, and he had to do it himself.

His grandfather walked into the house at last, singing some song about "ain't misbehaving." Michael walked his Honda out to the street as quietly as he could. He waited until he was out of sight of the house before he started the bike.

He was feeling better now, more like himself. *Almost human* were the words that came to mind. It sounded like a joke Sam would make. For some reason, right now Michael didn't find it funny.

He revved his bike and sped on down the highway.

He had to find Star.

What a night!

Lucy sat down on her bed. She hoped she could sleep. She certainly was exhausted enough. How much could happen to a person in just one day? With her two sons Lucy was sure she'd find out.

And then there was Max. She wished he hadn't felt so strongly that he had to impress her. She liked him when he was just being natural and easygoing, like the first night they had met.

Of course, there was a good possibility that Max was a thing of the past already, with the way she had run out on their dinner and all. She had called him up at the restaurant as soon as she'd made sure everything was all right with Sam, but she didn't think Max exactly understood her excuse. Oh, he had been polite enough and everything. Max was always polite. Then again, perhaps her real problem was that even she didn't completely believe her excuse. *Let's face it, Lucy Emerson, dating freaks you out. And let's not even think about commitment!*

"Mom?"

She looked up. Sam stood in the door.

"Can I sleep in here with you tonight?"

"In here?" Lucy replied, a bit surprised.

"Do you mind?" Sam asked meekly. "It was a *real* scary comic book."

She looked at her son and smiled. It was for moments like this that she'd never give up her boys. Maybe Max was right and she was a lioness after all.

"Okay," she said.

Sam plopped down on the bed next to her.

What was that smell?

"Have you been eating pizza?" she asked. "You smell like garlic."

The cave looked empty.

Michael walked slowly inside. It seemed brighter in here now, but maybe it was only his eyes adjusting to the moonlight.

The empty wine bottle from the night before sat in the middle of the floor. Michael walked over and picked it up. He lifted the top of the bottle to his nose and sniffed. He smelled a sour, acrid odor. It didn't smell like wine.

"I'm over here, Michael." Star's voice came out of the shadows.

Michael looked in the corner of the lobby. Star sat there on a long couch, Laddie asleep in her lap. She gently moved the boy onto the couch beside her, careful not to wake him. She stood, covering Laddie's shoulders with his old Army band coat to keep him warm, then walked across the room to Michael.

He was surprised when he saw the look on her face. Star looked every bit as upset and frightened as Michael felt. He put his hands on her shoulders and looked deep into her eyes.

"What's happening to me, Star?"

Star's lower lip trembled, as if she might start crying at any moment.

"Michael," she whispered.

He had to kiss her. Their lips met, again and again. Michael had kissed other girls before, but it had never been like this. He kissed her forehead, her neck, her shoulder. She did the same to him, and her kisses felt like ice and fire, freezing and burning in the same instant. And every kiss left him wanting more.

As they kissed, Star was leading him across the room. To where? Then Michael remembered. As David gave him the grand tour of the place the night before, the Lost Boy had pointed to curtained nooks around the walls: the "sleeping quarters." Star's and Laddie's cubicles were away from the others, over near the old wrought-iron elevator. That's where Star was taking him now.

Michael pulled aside the curtain and followed her inside.

What was that?

Michael awoke with a start. It was one of the strangest noises he had ever heard. Although, at the same time, there had been something about it that he knew from somewhere else.

It took him a moment to remember. The noise, heard while he was still half asleep, had been disorienting. It sounded as if a great wind had rushed through the cave, bringing with it the sound of wings, flapping against the breeze, and another noise—

Where was he? It was only after he saw the sleeping form of Star next to him that he remembered about the night before. What was happening? He had come back to the Lost Boys' cave to find out. But he realized now that he had come here for another reason as well: to be with Star.

They had slept together the night before. It was what he had really wanted, even though he couldn't admit it to himself until now. They had fallen asleep together, for a few hours of peaceful dreams rather than nightmares, until Michael woke to the wind and the sound of wings. And the whispering. That was the other noise, the one he remembered from the night before. The whispering outside Grandpa's house; it was the same high-pitched, eerie sound.

He heard voices out in the Lobby. The Lost Boys were back.

Star slept next to him on the mattress. He gently shook her shoulder. She didn't move. He shook her a little harder.

"I have to talk to you," he urged.

"Have to sleep," Star replied groggily.

He nudged her again. They really needed to talk. He should have gotten an explanation from her first thing last night, but when he had seen her, he could only think of kissing her, of holding her—

Well, last night was over. He had to find out what was happening to him, what he could do to save himself.

He shook Star again.

"Have to sleep, Michael," Star repeated. "Tonight . . . at the . . . Boardwalk."

She barely got the last word out before she fell again into a deep sleep.

He felt as if he wanted to sleep as well. But he had to get up. The first light of dawn was showing through the cracks above. He had to move, to act, if he was going to find any way out of this. He climbed back into his clothes and pushed past the curtain into the lobby.

Laddie still slept on the old couch. There was no sign of David or the others.

Twenty-three

Michael parked his Honda next to the garage. He was too tired to put it away.

His mother sat on the porch swing, drinking coffee. Michael's hopes sank. He had figured, if he got back early enough, he would have been able to sneak inside without anybody seeing him.

His mother looked expectantly down at him as he trudged up the sidewalk. He wondered if there was any way out of this. Maybe if he moved fast enough, he still wouldn't have to talk.

"Hi," his mother called as he climbed the steps. He nodded and kept on walking.

"What's the matter, Michael?" Mom asked. "Aren't we friends anymore?"

Michael slowed down. It looked as though he'd have to talk, after all.

"Sure," he managed.

His mother frowned. "Does that mean we are, or we aren't, friends?"

He nodded his head wearily. "We are."

"Then let's act like friends." She leaned forward in her chair. "Let's talk."

What could he say? Michael couldn't think of a thing. This was not the right time for a big discussion. Maybe after he got some sleep—

"If there's a girl," Mom prompted, "we could talk about her."

He just couldn't deal with this.

"I'm tired now." He stepped toward the door.

"Wait a minute, kiddo."

Michael stopped. He knew that tone of voice.

"Mom," he said slowly, "I have more serious things on my mind right now than school and girls. Things I've got to deal with myself—"

"Things I wouldn't understand," his mother added softly.

Michael took a step toward the door. His mother tugged at her ear and tried to smile.

"We haven't even gotten around to *this* yet!"

He blinked. What?

Oh. The earring. Michael was too tired now to try to explain anything. He walked down the hall and into the kitchen, leaving his mother behind. He wondered absently if he'd be able to eat any real food today. He hoped so, but just to be safe, he'd have to eat it when he was alone.

The kitchen was crowded. Sam was eating cereal and reading one of his comic books, while Grandpa poured himself a cup of coffee over by the sink. Sam looked Michael straight in the eye when he came in the room. Michael looked away. He wished his brother would give with one of his smartass remarks. Anything would be better than Sam looking at him like that.

Grandpa nodded in his direction. "Looks like I wasn't the only one got lucky last night."

Michael tried to grin but failed. What could he say? He wished he could tell Grandpa the truth.

Sam crunched his cereal right under Michael's nose. It made him feel a little nauseous. He glanced down at the comic that Sam was reading. It was a horror book. On the second page, two men had surprised a vampire in its coffin and were busy pounding a stake into its heart.

Michael didn't feel like staying in the kitchen anymore.

This was probably a silly thing to do. Lucy decided she wanted to do it, anyway. So she and Sam piled in the Land Rover and stopped in this nice little store in town to pick up a bottle of wine. Lucy wrote a quick note of apology on the spot and taped it to the bottle. Now was the time to deliver it, in person, to Max's place.

She stopped the Rover when she got to the mailbox. Yep. This was the address she had written down. It was quite a place, a nice little house built right on the ocean cliffs. It was set back from the road, too, by its own private bridge over a ravine. She guessed Max really could afford that Dom Perignon, after all.

"That's it?" Sam asked.

"Yeah," she said, ever so slightly in awe. "Not bad, huh?"

She grabbed the bottle of wine as she opened the door. She looked at Sam and pointed at the note.

"This is an apology for running out on Max last night." Her finger swiveled to point at Sam. "Actually *you* should be making the apology!"

Her son grinned sheepishly. Satisfied that she had made her point, she left the car carrying the bottle. This whole thing was a bit impetuous on her part—she still didn't know Max all that well, after all—but it made her feel good to do it. Even though she had tried to explain things to Max the night before, she had felt it hadn't been enough. For one thing, she had been so upset last night, she was afraid she hadn't been coherent. And she had been upset for more than the obvious reason, an understandable anger at Sam for ruining her evening. She was really more upset at herself from running away so quickly from a perfectly reasonable dinner date.

But now that she had set her mind to do it, her second reason seemed even more important: Max had been so nice to her, she wanted to do something nice in return.

She walked over the bridge to a wooden gate that swung into the driveway. She pushed at the iron handle, but the gate was locked. Max must be away, opening that second store of his. She realized then that part of her had wanted to give Max the wine in person. Oh, well. With Max's schedule she should have expected this. The apology business wasn't going to be quite as easy as she had first hoped. She walked a couple paces back toward the Rover.

"I'd better leave this on the front porch," she called to Sam, "or somebody's just going to take it."

She turned back to face the gate. Lucy decided to climb over and hike across the lawn.

As she approached the house she saw Max's dog sleeping on the porch.

"Hi, Thorn!" she called.

The dog looked up and jumped for her with a roar.

It took a second for Lucy to register what was happening. The dog leapt forward, growling.

Thorn was attacking her! She got a glimpse of bared teeth, saliva dripping from the corners of the mouth, the dog coming for her fast.

She turned and ran.

"Mom!" Sam had jumped from the car.

Lucy felt the wine bottle slip from her fingers, heard it smash on the sidewalk behind her. The dog sounded as if it were right at her heels.

She ran back to the gate, grabbed the top wooden slat, and jumped over in one motion.

Thorn banged into the fence behind her with a crash.

Lucy looked back, trying to catch her breath. Thorn tore at the wood with his claws, barking and growling. He would tear down the fence to get to her.

Lucy stood up. She realized she had skinned her knee in the fall. She didn't feel any pain, though, at least not yet.

Sam was by her side. "You okay, Mom?"

She shook her head, trying to clear it. She wasn't sure exactly how she felt, scared or foolish.

"I'm okay, Sam," she said, wishing she really believed it. "I'm okay."

Twenty-four

Sam knew what Thorn looked like when the dog had attacked his mother. That was why he got to the comic-book store even before it had opened for the day. He had to talk to the Frogs.

He explained the situation to them as soon as the brothers let him inside.

"And the dog came after her," he concluded, "just like the Hounds of Hell in *Vampires Everywhere!*"

Edgar nodded his head solemnly. "We've been aware of some very serious vampire activity in this town for a long time."

Alan agreed, equally solemn. "Santa Carla has become a haven for the Undead."

"As a matter of fact," Edgar added, "we're almost certain that ghouls and werewolves occupy high positions at City Hall."

Alan put a reassuring hand on Sam's shoulder. "Kill your brother and you'll feel a lot better."

Sam looked back and forth between the Frogs. They still weren't hearing what he was trying to tell them. He decided to make another attempt.

"My brother," Sam insisted, "is not a bloodsucker yet." He pointed to the vampire comic he'd brought along for this very reason. "Look. It says here that if you kill the head vampire, then all the half vampires will return to normal." He looked up at the Frogs in triumph. "If my brother's a vampire, believe me, as weird as he's acting, he's only half. I mean, Michael always acted sort of weird to begin with.''

Edgar considered this, reading the comic over Sam's shoulder. After a moment's pause he asked, ''Does he know who did this to him?''

''No,'' Sam admitted. At least, he hadn't told Sam if he did. Michael seemed so confused, Sam doubted he really knew anything about what was going on.

''Then kill him,'' Edgar replied, ''or we will.''

This, Sam thought, is what happens when you ask for advice from Rambo look-alikes. What could he tell them that would make them change their minds?

''Listen,'' he said at last, ''this whole thing started after we came to Santa Carla. My mom went to work at Max's Video. Now, the dog who went after her this morning belongs to Max.

''Here.'' He flipped rapidly through the comic book in front of him. ''This'll change your mind. Listen to this.'' He found the right page and began to read aloud.

'' 'Remember, gentle readers, vampires require a daytime protector—a guardian—to watch over them as they sleep. Fierce dogs—the Hounds of Hell—are often employed for this very purpose!' ''

Sam looked up from the comic book, chilled by a sudden thought.

''What if my mother is dating the head vampire?''

The Frogs stared back at him. For the first time since he had gotten here, they seemed truly interested. Sam decided to push his advantage.

''You could nail him,'' he continued, ''and save Santa Carla. Truth, Justice, and the American Way triumphs, thanks to you!''

Edgar nodded again, but this time there was real determination in his head shake.

''We'll check Max out.''

Alan smiled grimly at his side. ''My brother and I are

on a mission to destroy all vampires''—he paused signifi-
cantly—''including your brother, if we have to.''

Now the Frogs were talking business. And, thankfully,
they had moved Michael down to an ''if'' on their kill list.
Maybe Sam could actually get them to save Michael, after
all. Now it was time to get technical. If his brother was
going to get rescued, he'd need to know as many of their
vampire-killing secrets as possible.

Sam leaned back against a comic bin. ''Exactly how
many vampires have you actually destroyed?''

The two brothers glanced at each other uncomfortably.

''To the present date?'' Alan asked.

''All together?'' Edgar added.

''Uh,'' Alan admitted, ''zero.''

Zero? What were these guys talking about, then? Sam
decided he should demand an explanation when the store's
front door slammed open.

It was the Surf Nazis. Or at least some of them. The boy
and girl who had been ripping off comics in there the other
day didn't seem to be with them. They pushed their way
into the store, knocking over a comics display on their way
in. The Mohawked guy in the lead stared down at the Frog
Brothers.

''You seen Greg or Shelly?'' he demanded.

''Who?'' Edgar replied.

''Greg and Shelly,'' the Nazi replied. Sam realized he
must be talking about the two gang members who weren't
with them.

Neither Edgar nor Alan replied.

''You know who I'm talking about!'' the Nazi demanded.

''Haven't seen any shoplifters,'' Alan replied coolly,
''till you walked in.''

The Mohawked punk pushed against Edgar.

''I think you're lyin' about seein' Greg.''

Edgar didn't move. The punk turned to look at the rest
of the gang. Sam could feel it getting tense in here.

"I think he's lyin'." He whipped his hand out, sending a whole row of comics to the floor. The other Surf Nazis laughed. The first Surf Nazi started tossing comics out of the bins, and the rest of the gang followed, plucking comics from everywhere. A pair of them flipped over a comic rack. The Surf Nazis whistled and cheered. It looked to Sam like they were going to trash the whole store.

Edgar and Alan jumped over the counter. Edgar ducked down below for a second, then came back up armed with a slingshot. He aimed for the Mohawked Nazi who'd started it all.

He fired. The pellet tore away half of the surfer's hair. That stopped the rest of them, right there.

Everybody froze. The surf punks watched the Frogs. Edgar kept his slingshot aimed at the guy with half a Mohawk. And Sam watched both of them, wishing that sometime in the future his life would get a little less dramatic.

Edgar fired again. The second missile whizzed past the Mohawk's head, the pellet neatly ripping out the punk's earring. Sam was amazed. A shot like that was almost impossible!

The Surf Nazis screamed together and ran from the store.

Edgar lowered the shotgun and allowed himself a grin. He looked at Sam for approval. Sam considered leaving that instant and talking to the Frogs after he calmed back down; say, in a year or two.

"Hey," Edgar remarked casually, "just because a Marine hasn't seen combat doesn't mean he still isn't a Marine."

A Marine? Sam swallowed. Well, maybe that was what Michael needed. He had a feeling, once he called in these Marines, that there'd be no calling them back.

That's when the Frogs' parents wandered in. They smiled at everybody like they were stoned. They smiled that way every time Sam saw them. Apparently the fact that somebody had just trashed their store didn't bother them in the least. It probably gave them something to do with their day, besides getting stoned.

Sam waited patiently while the Frog Brothers described what happened to the store to their parents. Once they were done with that, they and Sam had plans to make. Plans he hoped were enough to save his brother from a life (or was it death?) of bloodsucking.

Twenty-five

It was funny, Lucy thought, how things could change with time. Toward the end of her marriage to Lance, she couldn't stand being in the kitchen. The simple sight of a pot on the stove would make her depressed as anything. Later, during the divorce, her feelings changed again, and the thought that she ever cooked for him would make her as angry as she had ever been. Cooking had become a symbol of everything that had gone wrong, both in Lucy's marriage and her life.

Now, though, it was completely different. The kitchen here at her father's was a bright, roomy place. She enjoyed putting things together again, finding new ways to be creative with old recipes. When she made things in the kitchen now, it helped relax her, draining the tension out of her days. She no longer cooked for that bastard of a husband who kept her at home while he played around. Now she cooked for herself, and the fact that her sons and her father ate it, and usually liked it, was an added bonus.

Tonight, though, she felt especially good. It wasn't the particular dinner. She thought her spaghetti sauce was special, but it wasn't all that difficult to make.

The difference, Lucy admitted, was a man. Max had found her note on the broken wine bottle, had even guessed that Thorn had chased her, and apologized for the dog's overzealousness. He had invited her out again that night by way of his own apology. She had countered with an invitation to a home-cooked meal. Max had laughed. What could he do, he said, but accept?

Now her whole family could meet the new man in her life. It made cooking even better. With Max coming to dinner, the specter of her husband had completely vanished from the kitchen.

Her father wandered into the kitchen and methodically inspected Lucy's handiwork, lifting the lids from one pot after another.

"Smells good," Grandpa said. "When do we eat?"

Lucy smiled at her father. "I told Max eight o'clock."

"Max?" Her father made a face. "You mean, we're having company again?"

"Again?" Lucy tapped her wooden spoon on the edge of the sauce pot. "Dad, you haven't had any company in this house since Mom died eight years ago."

"Right." He nodded his head emphatically. "And now we're having company *again*." He took the lid off another of the pots and sniffed appreciatively. "I'll take mine to go."

Michael walked into the room.

He was wearing all new clothes. Pretty flashy too. He certainly was a handsome boy. Of course, she was his mother. What else would she think?

She did wish, though, that he wouldn't wear his dark glasses all the time. Oh, she realized that it was just a teenage affectation and certainly no weirder than a lot of things she wore when she was sixteen. Still, he had such nice eyes! She wished he'd show them off a little more. And she really didn't like that earring he wore. It made him look too much like a member of that motorcycle gang she had seen out at Max's Video that night. She hoped Michael wasn't getting involved with the wrong crowd. With the new job and everything, she'd gotten a little out of touch with her family. She and Michael would have to sit down and have a long talk about this tomorrow.

Her son nodded at her as he surveyed the vast array of utensils covering the stove and counter. Maybe she should

try to talk to him a little now. It looked like her relationship with Max might get serious. She really wanted to
discuss the possibility of a new man in her life with both
her sons.

"Max is coming for dinner, Michael," Lucy said casually. "I'd like you to meet him."

"Can't," Michael mumbled. "Got plans of my own."

How could she hope to discuss anything with him when
he wouldn't even talk to her? She had had just about
enough of this sort of thing.

"There's only three weeks left of summer, Michael,"
she replied curtly. "Things are going to change around
here when school starts."

Michael turned and left the kitchen without another
word. Lucy sighed. What was she going to do with that
boy?

His mother would never understand! Michael could feel
the anger boiling up inside him. How could anybody
understand? Michael sighed. Maybe he was being a little
hard on her. He had been awfully angry lately. Ever since
the change came over him, it seemed like he was getting
mad at everything. But then, he had every reason to be
angry, didn't he?

He opened the front door. A kind of nerdy guy around
his mother's age, wearing glasses and a tie, smiled at him.

"Hey," the guy with the tie said. "How ya doing?
Michael, right?"

Uh-oh. This must be the new love of his mother's life.
Michael always thought she had had better taste.

"Yeah," he replied with a nod. "Max, right?"

They stood and looked at each other for a moment.
Michael wondered what this guy wanted from him.

Max cleared his throat. "Listen," he said. "You're the
man of the house, Michael. I'm not coming in unless you
invite me."

Oh, no. Now this guy was using some sort of "psychological reinforcement" on him, making him feel important by calling Michael "the man of the house." Michael had learned all about this sort of thing in his psych course last year. He bet his mother put Max up to this too. What did they think he was, some sort of kid?

Max stood there, staring and smiling. Well, Michael thought, if I don't do something soon, I'm going to have to look at this geek all night.

"Come in, come in," Michael said at last. "I'm inviting you."

"Thank you very much." Max stepped into the foyer and looked surprised to see Michael pass him going out the door. What did the guy think, that Michael was going to spend the whole evening talking to him?

"See ya!" he called back as he walked down the steps.

He had to get to the Boardwalk and meet Star. Only then could he find out what was really happening.

Michael passed a bright red sports car on his way out to the garage, a brand-new Corvette. God, he thought, for a nerd he has a nice set of wheels. Maybe Michael had been too hasty. The total loser his mother was dating might have hidden depths.

He got his motorcycle out and drove out quickly to the main road. It was another beautiful evening. The cool air felt good on his face and hands. He was alive again for the first time since he had left Star. Days were getting to be a real drag.

He only really felt comfortable at night.

Twenty-six

There! Lucy smacked her lips in quiet triumph. The sauce was just about right, and everything else was finally in order. It was too bad Michael wasn't going to stay around, but she supposed Max could meet him later. And she was hoping there would be a later. Lucy didn't know quite what was wrong, but every time she and Max tried to get together, it never quite worked out. That's why she wanted tonight to be different, a perfectly planned evening where nothing could go wrong.

"Hello."

Lucy jumped a foot, startled by the closeness of the voice. She turned around to see Max smiling at her. Michael must have let him in. Didn't he know that sneaking up on people could scare the wits out of them?

"Is something wrong?" Max asked when he saw her expression. "Is it okay for the guest to see the food before dinner?"

Lucy laughed. And just where did he get that idea? She replied dryly, "You're thinking of the groom not seeing the bride before the wedding."

"Oh, right," Max agreed solemnly. "I always get those two confused."

Lucy shook her head at his remark, but she was still grinning. Men! She picked up the plate of garlic bread and carried it out into the dining room. Max followed her.

She put the plate on the dining room table, looking at the place setting with a critical eye. She had had Sam set the table, and as usual, he had been more fast than neat. She'd have to straighten things up a bit.

She felt Max's arms around her. It was a little forward of him in a way, and yet it felt right. His nose nuzzled gently against her neck. She turned around to face him, half thinking to protest his advances. But his face was so close. For a second Lucy forgot to breathe. He was going to kiss her! Their lips met for an instant.

"Mom!"

She pushed out of Max's embrace. Sam was standing at the other side of the dining room table, next to two other boys that she had never seen before. The two newcomers seemed to be around Sam's age, although they both looked much more serious than her son. Maybe she got that impression because they were both dressed in Army fatigues.

Sam waved at his two companions. "These are *my* dinner guests. Edgar and Alan. The Frog Brothers."

"Ah—" Lucy began, a bit discombobulated. Why hadn't Sam said anything about inviting his friends? "I didn't know you were having guests. . . ."

Sam looked downcast. He looked away from his mother to study the dining room's hardwood floor.

"Well," he said slowly, "if we're in your way, we can just eat peanut butter out of the jar in the kitchen."

What was Sam trying to do—make her look like the world's worst mother in front of Max?

"No, no," she hastily assured Sam. "There's plenty for everybody." She looked up at her date, who seemed to be watching this whole drama with a certain bemused interest.

"Oh, Max," she added, "this is Sam and—uh—the Frog Brothers."

Lucy bit her lip while Max and the boys studied one another. She had wanted this little dinner at home to be perfect. Why did she have the feeling that it was already out of control?

It was so obvious. Couldn't his mother tell that Max was a vampire?

Well, of course, Sam and the Frogs knew all about it because of what had happened with the dog. His mother was the only one who hadn't gotten around to reading "Hounds of Hell" in the *Vampires Everywhere* comic, so there was probably no way for her to make the connection. Sam wondered if there was some way he could get her to look at the story without being too obvious; say, leaving the book open to "Hounds of Hell" on her pillow. Knowing his mother, though, she'd probably just close the comic and tell Sam to keep his books in his own room, please. That was the problem with mothers. They could be very difficult at times. Sam and the Frogs would have to get definite proof of Max's vampirism before his mom would believe them. But then, that was why all three of them had joined Mom and Max for dinner.

Lucy had the Frogs pull up a couple extra chairs, and they all sat down to eat.

"This looks terrific, Lucy." Max beamed. His mother smiled back. Gee, did his mother fall for that kind of stuff?

"Boy!" his mom said after a minute. "Somebody around here sure has bad breath!"

All right! Maybe his mother had noticed something, after all! Sam hated to think what a vampire's breath really smelled like, with all that blood drinking and all. He and the Frogs looked at Max. Would he reveal his true nature now?

His mother pushed Nanook's head off her lap. Oh, no. She couldn't mean the dog.

"Nanook," she said, "stop breathing on me."

She did mean the dog. "C'mere, Nanook," Sam called. Come to think of it, why wasn't the dog growling at Max? Could the vampire have cast some sort of spell over the animal?

The Frogs looked at each other. Their disappointment was obvious. They had thought they had caught the vampire, but now—

Still, the three of them had not yet begun to fight. It was time to take definite action.

It was time for Plan A.

Sam pointed to Max's plate of spaghetti.

"How about a little Parmesan cheese on that?"

"Okay, Sam." Max grinned in his direction. Shouldn't a vampire's teeth be sharper than that? "Thanks."

Sam sprinkled some grated cheese onto Max's spaghetti. He glanced at Edgar and Alan. The Frogs nodded smugly. They knew Plan A was under way.

They all watched Max as he wound the spaghetti around his fork, then brought the fork to his mouth.

He gagged before he could even start chewing.

"Max!" Lucy called from the other side of the table. "What's wrong?"

"It's—it's garlic!" He sputtered. "I like garlic, but—"

"Quick!" Sam urged. "Drink some water."

With that he spilled a glass of water in Max's lap.

"Hey!" Max jumped from his seat. "Easy!" He tried to wipe off the mess in his lap with a napkin.

Sam leaned toward him. "Does it burn?"

"Burn?" Max looked at Sam as if he were crazy. "Are you kidding? It's freezing!"

"Max!" His mother was on her feet now too. "I'm so sorry!"

Uh-oh, Sam thought, this guy was smooth. Two clear tests and he still hadn't shown a single sign of his vampirism. He was going to be tougher to crack than they thought. Sam glanced at Edgar. Edgar nodded back.

Yes, it was definitely time for Plan B.

Edgar moved his chair slightly away from the table, then casually leaned back until his hand touched the light switch.

The room went dark.

"Now what?" his mother asked.

"Must be a circuit breaker," Sam said. It was time to

get to work. He heard chairs squeak across the hardwood floor as Edgar and Alan moved to join him.

"He's not glowing!" Edgar whispered in his ear.

But Sam was ready for the final test. "Hit the lights again," he whispered back.

The lights went on, and Sam held a mirror against Max's face.

Max yelled and jumped away. He laughed nervously as soon as he realized what he had done. He looked to Lucy.

"Scared by my own reflection," he explained.

But his mother wasn't amused in the least.

"Sam!" she demanded. "What's gotten into you tonight?"

Max stood behind his chair at the table. He frowned at the boys.

"I think I know what's going on here."

"You do?" Edgar replied.

Max nodded. Sam swallowed, hard. They had been too obvious. Maybe they should have been better prepared. What would they do if they had to face a vampire's wrath?

"Sure," Max said. "I understand what you're thinking, Sam. But you're wrong."

"I am?" Sam replied. Did Max really know what he was thinking?

"Yeah," Max said. "I'm *not* trying to replace your dad—or steal your mom. I just want to be your friend."

Sam stared at the older man for a long moment.

Gee, maybe Max wasn't a vampire, after all.

Lucy walked with Max to the door. Thanks to the boys, his suit was soaking wet.

"I'm really sorry, Max," she said.

But he smiled that smile of his. "Our batting average isn't very good, is it?" He chuckled softly. "So far we're zero for two."

Lucy ran a hand through her hair. "I don't understand Sam. He's just not like this."

Max's smile vanished. "Boys Sam's age need a good deal of discipline," he said softly, "or they walk all over you."

What did Max mean by that remark? "He doesn't walk all over me!" she retorted brusquely. Max hardly knew her children at all.

Max put his hand on her shoulder. "Look. I don't want to fight with you, Lucy. Come on. Let's give it one more try." His smile came back, encouraging. "Dinner at my house tomorrow night? I'm cooking."

Lucy said yes. Max kissed her lightly, a longer, more lingering kiss than before, then turned and was gone. She watched him get into his car and drive off into the night.

She wondered for a moment if Max had been right about disciplining her boys. Heaven knew Michael had been acting up lately. And what Sam had done tonight! Maybe the move to Santa Carla had been tougher on both of them than she imagined.

She thought for a moment about her and Max raising the boys together. It wasn't an unpleasant fantasy. She turned away from the door and went back inside.

There was something about Max. Something magnetic. She really wanted to do a lot more of this kissing.

As she walked back into the dining room she saw Grandpa peering out of his taxidermy room. She bet he had sat there all night, watching. She swore, sometimes her father could be so strange.

Twenty-seven

The Lost Boys had gone out, but this evening they hadn't asked her to come along. Star knew what that meant. She and Laddie had sat on a sofa and watched silently as David and the others got ready.

Only Paul had tried to cheer her up. Goofy Paul. He'd frowned back at her, then thrust out his lower lip like he was pouting. She hadn't thought she looked like that! She had wanted to throw something at him.

All the Lost Boys were so different. Marco was always mysterious; Dwayne a little awkward. Paul was the comedian of the group. He'd do anything to get her to laugh. From the time she had first gotten to know them, David had fascinated her, but Paul had always been the one she could talk to. She sometimes wondered just why that was.

Before she and Laddie had come here, Paul had been the newest member of the gang. She thought that perhaps, more than the others, Paul still remembered what it meant to be lonely.

And then Paul asked if she was worried about Michael.

Star hadn't known she was that obvious. Paul told her not to worry. Being obvious was part of her charm.

But he couldn't cheer her up. Not now. Not anymore. She wanted to get angry instead. When she had first met the Lost Boys, everything had been so simple. Then Michael came into her life. Now Star didn't know what she wanted.

Paul had left with a wave, telling her not to worry. They were all going to live happily ever after.

Star stared down at the old hotel carpet. Laddie called her name, but she was too upset to answer. She had never felt this alone in her entire life.

What could she do?

Michael couldn't find Star anywhere. He should never have left her this morning without getting an explanation. She had told him she'd meet him on the Boardwalk. But he never realized, before tonight, just how long the Boardwalk was. It ran the entire length of downtown Santa Carla, from the amusement rides over to the pier, maybe ten long city blocks. And every inch of every block was crammed with people!

He kept coming back to that place, near the bandstand, where he had first seen her listening to rock and roll. That had been—what?—only four nights ago? Those four nights seemed longer than the whole rest of his lifetime. In those nights he had met a girl finer than any he ever could have imagined before he came to this place. And those same nights might have damned him, changing him into something that was no longer human.

Where was Star? His hopes had risen half a dozen times as he had seen girls in the distance with long, curly hair. But as he approached each one she had shown her face— the wrong face—or moved in a way that Star would never move. Where could she have gone? She wouldn't desert him now. He needed her too much. She knew what was happening to him and what could be done to change it. And, he had to admit, he wanted to see her more than he had ever wanted to see anyone, to touch her hair, to hear her laugh. He knew if he could just be with her, things would get better. Whatever happened to him, she held his happiness.

So he came back to the bandstand again. There was no band there tonight. Everyone was crowded around the other Boardwalk amusements: miniature golf, the pinball machines and electronic games.

There, in the middle of the crowd, were the Lost Boys. Michael looked around wildly. The sight of David and his gang made him even more frantic. They had done this thing to him, but only Star could save him!

He couldn't see her anywhere. Star was still nowhere around.

David had his back to Michael. None of the Lost Boys had seen him. They were too busy watching the kids play the row of penny-arcade machines. The air was filled with the clang of pinball scores and the electronic beeps of video action. Somehow all the noise made Michael even angrier.

He rushed up to David and grabbed his shoulders, spinning him around.

"Where is she?" he demanded, shouting to be heard over the music.

"Hey!" David pulled his hands back, as if he were surrendering. "Take it easy!"

But Michael wasn't buying David's friendly act anymore.

"Where's Star, David?"

David looked back at Michael, no smile on his face, no fun anymore. From here on in, David's expression said that this was serious.

"If you ever want to see Star again," he said, "you better come with us."

He shouted to the other Lost Boys to follow him. They left the Boardwalk and got on their motorcycles. Michael ran to get his. David waited a minute for him to catch up, then all five of them took off down the beach road.

Michael had thought they'd go back to the cave, but David led them to a spot in the woods instead. The Lost Boys pulled up and parked so that they would be hidden from the road. Then, one by one, Marco, Dwayne, and Paul climbed into the trees.

David waited for him. He pointed to a tree for Michael to climb.

But Michael wasn't playing games anymore.

"What is this, David?" he asked.

David looked back at him, just as serious.

"You're one of us now—aren't you?"

What did David mean by that? It sounded like he was both welcoming him to the gang and threatening him at the same time.

David shook his head. "You'll never see Star again if you're not."

So they had trapped him into following them, and now David trapped him into climbing. Michael wondered where this would end. What did they really want from him?

In the end, though, it didn't matter. David's trap was a good one, its invisible bars as solid as steel.

David shinnied up the tree, waving for Michael to follow. Michael did as he was told. No matter what happened, he had to see Star again.

It was a big old oak, with sturdy branches spreading close enough to each other that the climb was easy. They both climbed about halfway up the oak, where the branches started to thin. David climbed onto the branch next to Michael. The branch didn't bend at all. For an instant Michael was surprised, until he remembered last night, when he had floated, weightless, through his bedroom window.

"Look there." David pointed. The trees ended at a slim strip of sand, and out on that beach was a small group of teenagers around a fire. They sat out there drinking beer and passing around a joint, laughing and talking, completely unaware that they were being watched. Michael realized after a minute that they were another gang, one he had seen the day he had worked cleaning up the beach: the Surf Nazis.

David nodded to the other Lost Boys.

And they began to change.

It was a moonless night, the first one all week, and Michael couldn't clearly see what was happening. He did see David raise his arms above his head. Something happened to his arms, or the clothes around his arms. David pushed away from the tree and flew.

The other three Lost Boys left their trees as well, and the four swooped down over the camp fire. Their flight was almost soundless, the only noise a strange, high whispering sound. The Surf Nazis looked up at the approaching noise. Somebody screamed.

Michael watched from the tree, fascinated despite himself, as the Lost Boys flew around the confused and frightened surfers. This was what he was becoming. This was what David wanted him to be. And Star? Was she like this too? Did he have to become a Lost Boy to be with Star?

Michael could feel his heart beat.

It was all happening so fast, out there by the camp fire. A couple of the Surf Nazis had stood up and were trying to fight back, but wherever their fists flew, the Lost Boys had already left. The surfers staggered around drunkenly, looking as if they were shadowboxing with the fire.

Marco flashed into the middle of the fight. Something dark and wet was flowing from along a Nazi's shoulder and arm. Marco made a howling, animal sound.

The surfer with the Mohawk turned around, looking for some way to escape. But David was on top of him in a second.

"Hey, dude!" David screamed. "My beach, my wave!"

The Lost Boy's feet settled on the other guy's shoulder and ribs. The Nazi flailed at him, trying to shake him loose. David grabbed the surfer's arms. His face swept down toward the Mohawk.

Michael gasped.

David had bitten off the top of the Nazi's skull, Mohawk and all. Blood spurted from the wound as the Nazi screamed.

Michael turned away. He couldn't watch any more. They wanted him to act like them? No! Never!

The beat of his heart was loud in his ears. Michael closed his eyes. He was sweating despite the coolness of the night. He took a deep breath. He couldn't seem to get enough oxygen. The pounding in his head grew louder, threatening to cut out all other noise, all other sensation.

"Michael!"

He opened his eyes and looked to the others. David was calling to him. His pulse beat in his temples. The world flowed around him, rippling with his heartbeat.

It was like last night.

"Michael!"

The Lost Boys called his name.

"Michael!" It was a shout and a whisper.

"Michael!" He heard it through his ears. He heard it through his mouth and tongue and throat and stomach. He heard it deep inside his head, where something stirred and woke.

"Michael! Michael! Michael!"

Their chanting matched the pounding of his heart.

He was one of them now. He could fly from this tree and join them. They called for him to come. The pounding in his skull told him to go.

He knew what he needed.

He needed blood.

Michael shivered and closed his eyes. He turned away from the carnage on the beach. What was he thinking?

There were more screams from the fire below. The Lost Boys were tearing the surfers apart. Michael felt as if he were going to be sick.

He had to get out of here. It was time to climb down from his tree and get away on his bike, as far away as he could go. He placed his right foot on a lower branch.

His foot slipped. Michael gasped as he started to slide. He came down the tree fast, falling on a pile of leaves on the forest floor.

He laid there for a long moment, trying to catch his breath. He heard new sounds from over by the camp fire, different from the screaming he had heard before, sounds he didn't want to put a name to.

Then there was silence.

A moment later Michael heard the sound of footsteps moving across the leaves and twigs. The footsteps were coming toward him.

The Lost Boys came out of the shadows. They looked tired, but their faces were lit with little smiles of satisfaction. Their eyes glowed too. At first Michael thought it was some trick of the light, that the moon had finally broken through the clouds and was reflected in their eyes. But there was still no moon. Whatever made their eyes glow came from within.

David and the others walked up to Michael.

"Now you know who we are," he said quietly. "And who you are too."

No, Michael wanted to say. Not me. Not like you. He wanted to scream out his protests to these creatures, to deny any kinship to these monsters of the night. He opened his mouth, but the words never came out of his throat.

"You'll never grow old and you'll never die." David smiled reassuringly down at him. "But you must feed."

Michael's eyes were drawn back to the camp fire, back to the place where people no longer screamed.

The Lost Boys walked away.

Twenty-eight

The eyes were staring at him. Even in the darkness Sam knew they were there.

There was light reflected in those eyes. The bedroom door opened. Someone came in the room.

Something touched him.

"Aaaagh!" Sam screamed as he leapt for the light switch.

He flipped on the light. Michael stood over him, looking a little startled from Sam's scream.

Sam looked back over at the stuffed owl that had been watching him all night. He'd had enough of this. He got out of his bed and marched to the dresser from which the owl stared.

"I wish he'd stop giving me these things," Sam said to his brother. He grabbed the owl and opened the closet. Half a dozen other stuffed animals stared at him from the closet shelves. He tossed the owl in with the rest.

"I know everything," Michael said behind him. "I've seen everything. They—they took me . . ."

Sam turned around when he realized Michael had stopped talking. What did his brother mean? That he knew everything about vampires? He looked at Michael. He didn't look very happy.

Sam tried to think of some way to cheer his brother up. Maybe there was some solution in one of the vampire comics.

"Michael!" a girl's voice called from outside the window. "Michael!"

Both Sam and Michael rushed to the window to see what was going on. The moon had broken through the clouds, and its light showed a girl standing in the middle of the back yard. She looked up and waved at them.

Sam recognized her right away. "It's that girl from the Boardwalk." And the girl that you've been seeing, he thought to himself. He glanced at Michael. "Is she one of them?"

Michael looked back at him, miserable. "I think so."

"I have to talk to you!" the girl called. "Can I come up?"

"Sure!" Michael yelled. "Hold on!" He jumped away from the window and ran out of the room. He was almost to the stairs in a matter of seconds.

What was his brother doing? Didn't he know this girl was a vampire?

"She's one of them!" Sam yelled. "And don't tell me it doesn't make her a bad person!"

Sam's yell made him turn around.

Michael didn't have to go down the stairs. She suddenly appeared in the doorway to the bedroom, as if she had flown there. As if she were a vampire.

Michael was startled. Seeing Star here didn't bring the feeling of relief he'd expected. Maybe it was the way she came here, with her inhuman powers; maybe everything else that had happened to Michael, suddenly welling up inside him. Whatever it was, Michael looked at Star and found himself filled with anger.

"Do you know where David took me tonight, Star?" he shouted. "Do you?"

"Yes." Her face crumbled inward, as if she were about to cry. "And I'm to blame for it. If you hadn't met me"—she paused and took a ragged breath—"if I hadn't liked you"—her voice seemed to be shrinking with every word—"I tried to warn you—"

Seeing her like this almost made Michael's anger dissolve, almost but not quite. She was responsible for this. She admitted it.

"That night in the cave," he continued. "That wasn't wine they gave me to drink. It was David's blood!"

"You drank someone's blood?" Sam yelled.

"I'm one of them, Star!" Michael yelled. "I'm just like them!"

"Not yet!" Star shook her head. Her tears were gone. "You're like Laddie and me. We're not like the others, until . . ." Her voice trailed off.

"Until you've made your first kill!" Sam added helpfully. He had walked across the room after Michael had mentioned drinking blood. Now he stood just beyond Star.

"Sam!" Michael yelled. His brother was spouting nonsense from his comic books.

Star shook her head again. "He's right. You were supposed to be my first kill, Michael, but I couldn't. Not to you."

Michael looked at his brother. Something in one of his comic books was actually true? Then he looked up at Star.

"Then it's not too late for us?"

"It's not too late for you to be saved." Star smiled slightly, although her face was still full of sadness. "But each night . . . it becomes harder and harder for me to resist."

Michael thought of the pounding of his heart, and the need.

"I know," he answered in a low voice. "I've felt it."

Star leaned against the side of the door. "I'm weak. Soon I'll need—"

"To feed!" Sam added helpfully. He looked at the two of them and took a couple of quick steps away.

Michael looked at Star. She seemed so vulnerable, resting against the edge of the door, and so beautiful. Michael saw again why he had fallen for her in the first place. He wanted so much to help her.

He realized then that he was no longer angry.

He stepped forward and kissed her. Her lips were cool but not cold. She was still alive! They both were, and Michael was going to see to it that they stayed that way.

Star pushed away. She looked afraid.

"David's looking for me!" she exclaimed. "I have to go!"

Michael shook his head. "You're not going anywhere." He leaned past her to wave a "come here" to his brother. "Sam?"

Star was gone. Michael sensed it before he even turned back around. He hadn't even seen her go, but he knew she had fled, back through the window.

Michael ran to look out into the backyard.

"Star!" he called.

"Hey!" Sam leaned out of the window next to him. "Don't kill anybody until we get back to you!"

Star was gone. There was nothing outside but the sound of the crickets.

Finally Michael stepped back from the window. Sam was already across the room, dialing the phone.

"What are you doing?" Michael asked.

Sam smiled enigmatically. "I have connections."

Twenty-nine

The Frogs had arrived. Just as promised, they rode up on their bikes just after dawn, or as they put it, "Six hundred and thirty hours."

Sam opened the door as they marched up the steps. The Frog Brothers were dressed for war, complete with knapsacks, camouflage jackets, and green berets. They walked into the house.

"Okay," Edgar snapped. "Where's Nosferatu, the Prince of Darkness?"

"The nightcrawler," Alan added. "The bloodsucker."

"*El vampiro*," Edgar rejoined.

Sam turned to look upstairs.

"They're here, Michael!" he shouted.

His brother staggered down the stairs. Boy, did he look terrible! His skin was deathly pale behind his dark glasses. And Sam could swear his brother had lost ten pounds in the last couple days.

Edgar whistled as Michael continued his slow descent.

"This guy looks more like a zombie."

Alan shrugged his knapsack from his shoulders and reached inside it. He pulled out a sharpened stake.

"Should I run him through?" he asked his brother eagerly.

But Edgar was studying Michael. "I've only got one question for you," he said, "and I want an honest answer. Have you taken any human victims yet?"

Michael reached the bottom of the stairs.

"Of course not!" His voice was still surprisingly strong.

"If you're telling the truth," Edgar replied, "it means we can save you."

What were the Frogs implying?

"He's telling the truth!" Sam insisted. "Aren't you, Michael?"

Edgar nodded solemnly. "To free you we must destroy the leader of the vampires."

Michael nodded back. "David."

"I don't want names!" Edgar shouted militarily. "Just lead me to him. Where's their nest?"

"I'll take you," Michael replied.

Alan looked skeptical. "You can barely stand up. Besides"—he looked meaningfully at Edgar and Sam—"we can't trust you. You're practically one of them."

Michael leapt forward and grabbed Edgar's arm. How could his brother move so fast?

"I said, *I'll take you there*." Michael's voice had risen ever so slightly. "Nobody's going near Star without me. Understand?"

Edgar nodded rapidly. "Okay. Okay."

Michael released his grip. Edgar rubbed his arm. He looked at Alan.

"Vampires," Edgar said, "have such rotten tempers."

Sam had had enough of this infighting. He asked everybody if they were ready. Michael and the Frog Brothers looked at each other, but they all said yes.

Sam led them out through the back porch to the garage. Their grandfather was way off in the side yard with his pickup, pounding fence posts into the ground. Good, that meant that this was going to be even easier than Sam had imagined.

Sam opened the garage door as the other three piled in the car. Michael was the only one here old enough to drive, so, even in his wasted condition, he was behind the wheel. The Frogs were in the back. Sam jumped into the passenger seat.

Michael backed the '57 Chevy out of the garage with a squeal of tires. Grandpa looked up from his work.

"Grandpa!" Sam yelled very quickly. "Okay-if-we-borrow-the-car?"

Before Grandpa could answer, Michael had turned the car around and headed down the highway toward town.

Michael drove slowly down the back roads, trying to find the way. It looked different during the day, and he was so tired that he could barely think. It took him close to an hour before he found the cliff overlooking the cave.

But he found it. He parked the Chevy just beyond the Lost Boys' bikes, close to the stairs leading down to the caves. Edgar and Alan spent a long moment inventorying the contents of their knapsacks: two flashlights, two mallets, and thirty-six pointed stakes. That meant they could kill each of the Lost Boys nine times. Well, Michael thought, it was probably better that they were prepared. As long as they didn't get any ideas about Star, whatever they did was fine with Michael.

They all piled out of the car, Michael in the lead, ready to lead them down the stairs. Edgar ran up next to him.

"Just so you know," the Frog Brother began. "If you try to stop us, or vamp-out in any way, I'll stake you without thinking twice about it."

"Chill out, Edgar," Sam said right behind them.

"This is war, Sam," Alan replied. He walked up to his brother, who stood at the top of the rickety stairs.

The Frogs looked at each other and nodded once. They both made a thumbs-up gesture at exactly the same time and plunged double time down the stairs. Even Michael had to admit that their moves were pretty impressive. It was as if they had practiced this moment for weeks.

Dizzy. Michael suddenly felt as if his legs no longer had any muscle, and his bones were going to collapse beneath him. He stumbled and almost fell. Sam grabbed his arm and helped him to regain his balance.

This was getting worse. He didn't feel the change this way at night. After dark he could still move around and sometimes even forget what had happened to him. But the sunlight drained him. He could barely do anything during the day. All he wanted to do was sleep.

"Sam," Michael managed after he was sure he wouldn't fall. "If something happens to me . . . if I don't have the strength to go on, promise me you won't let them hurt Star."

Sam looked up at him, worry in his eyes. It looked like his little brother might finally be realizing how close to the edge Michael really was. Michael tried to smile but couldn't quite get it right.

Sam promised.

Together the two of them walked down the stairs. It took a while, but they made it. Edgar and Alan waited for them at the entrance to the cave. They said they had had a conference and decided to wait for their Intelligence Source before proceeding farther.

Michael realized they meant him. He wondered if the Frogs had just gone a bit chicken when they'd reached the darkened cave mouth. But Edgar and Alan ran into the cave as soon as Michael and Sam had caught up with them.

Michael and Sam followed the Frogs inside. Edgar and Alan hadn't gotten very far. They had stopped, open-mouthed, to gape at the lobby.

"Wow," Sam whispered beside him.

Michael had to admit it looked pretty impressive. He'd never seen the place in full daylight before. Even though few of the sun's rays seemed to make it directly down here, there was enough muted light to really get a sense of the size and colors in this old hotel. The sofas were covered with rich, dark, plush in blues and greens, a little worn here and there, but still in pretty good shape. The wine-colored rug was a little threadbare, too, with a few dark stains in the middle of the room. Michael didn't want to know what those stains were.

The light brought out more details in the mural along the wall and made the wrought-iron elevator look even larger and more imposing than it did at night. There was dust in the air, too, which gave everything a slightly yellowed look, as if you were looking at an old photograph.

But they were walking through this old photograph as well. It looked unreal, like a room stolen from another age.

A perfect place for vampires, Michael thought.

Edgar took out his flashlight. He flipped it on and directed its beam toward the nooks and crannies around the lobby walls.

"There's got to be a sleeping chamber around here somewhere," he muttered. He and Alan decided to inspect the walls for hidden passageways. Sam followed slowly, looking a bit overwhelmed by his surroundings.

Michael walked the other way, back toward the elevator, where he knew he would find Star.

He opened the curtain and found her asleep on her mattress. She looked so peaceful there, and so beautiful, her hair spread around her face like a dark halo. Michael knelt beside her. He shook her shoulder gently.

"Star," he called softly, "you're coming with me."

Her beautiful brown eyes snapped open in surprise.

"Michael?" she whispered. Her voice was weak, as if she had no strength left.

He should wrap her in something to keep her from getting a chill. He looked briefly through the pile of clothes in the corner, then found an old velvet cape on the floor. He took Star's hand, pulled her to a sitting position, and drew the cape over her shoulders.

"No," Star said.

Michael looked down at her. What was wrong? Didn't she want to get out of here?

"Take Laddie," she murmured weakly. "Please. Save Laddie first."

Michael opened his mouth to protest, but the look on Star's face kept any words from coming out. Her eyes pleaded with him to do what she asked. He smiled and kissed her lightly on the forehead, then went to get Laddie. How could he not do what she asked?

The boy slept on his couch, right beside Star's sleeping space. Michael leaned down, sliding his hands under the child.

It took all his strength to lift Laddie in his arms. Michael staggered under the weight. He had lost so much strength himself. He moved slowly, deliberately, carrying the boy from the cave, then up the never-ending stairs to the car. He had had the strength to do this sort of thing once. He would have to find the strength again.

Then, once he had brought Laddie to safety, he would be back for Star.

Thirty

"Hey, guys!"

Alan had found something! He waved for Edgar and Sam to come join him.

Sam was the last to arrive. Alan tapped him on the shoulder and pointed to an opening above the elevator cage.

"Feel it?" Alan urged. "Feel the draft?"

He was right. Sam could feel a cold, stiff breeze on his face. There had to be something up there!

Edgar shone the beam of the flashlight through the hole.

"It's an opening, all right. Let's try it. Somebody give me a boost."

Alan hoisted Edgar, then Sam did the same for Alan. Edgar reached down and pulled Sam in after them. Sam looked around the flashlight's beam. They were in a tunnel of some sort, the ceiling far enough above their heads so they could stand. Edgar turned the flashlight so that its beam shone down the tunnel's length. The beam faded in the distance.

"Let's go," Edgar ordered. The Frogs marched down the tunnel. Sam hurried to keep up, wishing he'd brought a flashlight of his own.

A fly buzzed near his ear. Sam tried to swat it aside, but it was followed by two or three more.

"That proves it!" Edgar declared with a note of triumph. "We're on the right trail. Flies and the undead go together like ham and eggs."

Alan opened a side compartment of his knapsack and

pulled out a can. So they had more in there than mallets and stakes. Sam hadn't even noticed the side compartments. He wondered what sort of anti vampire treatment this was.

Alan took off the can's plastic top and sprayed a cloud of gray smoke into the air. Sam choked and coughed at the same time. It was bug spray!

"Come on, men!" Edgar barked.

Sam ran to follow them, trying to breathe and get the bug spray taste out of his mouth at the same time. The flies started to buzz around him again a moment later, but he didn't complain.

There were worse things than flies.

Laddie woke up at the top of the stairs. He looked scared and confused. Michael shifted the blanket he carried the boy in so that it shaded Laddie's eyes.

The Chevy was only a few feet away, but Laddie had grown very heavy in his arms. Michael felt his legs wanting to give way again. He kept his knees stiff, and walked the last few feet straight legged until he reached the side of the car. He shifted Laddie's weight against the fender and managed to open the back door. Laddie had fallen back asleep. Michael doubted the kid had any more strength than Star or himself.

Michael pushed the sleeping child well into the car, then pulled his blanket around some more so that no sun would fall on his face. He closed the car door behind him and began the long walk back to the cave.

His right foot crumpled beneath him. Michael found himself down on one knee. He cursed. He swore at himself and his knee and his weakness. He pushed against the ground with his hands and managed to get the foot under him. He damned David and the Lost Boys, and what they had made him see and do. He stood and slowly walked. He had twisted his ankle slightly. Pain shot up his leg every time he put weight on the heel.

Shit, Michael thought, and kept on walking. He would rescue Star. His anger would keep him going.

It seemed like they'd been walking through this tunnel forever, nothing but stale air, darkness, and flies. Again and again Sam had hoped the passageway would end. Now he wasn't so sure.

The tunnel stopped just ahead, widening out into a cavern of some sort. The flies grew thicker around here again. Edgar picked up a dozen of them flying in his flashlight beam. There was a stiff, cold breeze coming from somewhere up ahead. It made Sam want to shiver. The breeze brought an odor with it, too; something foul, like the stench of rotting meat.

Sam wrinkled up his nose. "What's that smell?"

Edgar put a reassuring hand on his shoulder.

"Vampires, my friend," he said. "Vampires."

This was it, then. They had found their lair at last.

They stepped into the larger cave.

Michael limped across the lobby to the corner where Star slept. His ankle ached dully all the time now, and the pain had started his head pounding. If only he wasn't so tired. He'd feel better if he could rest for a few minutes. His anger had gotten him back down here. Now, though, he was even too tired to curse.

He made it, at last, to the corner where Star slept. He pulled back the curtain and looked down at her, still as beautiful as before. If only he could lie down next to her for a few minutes, rest a bit before trying to make it up to that car one more time. The mattress looked so inviting. Just a little while.

Star opened her eyes as he knelt beside her. She reached

out to touch his hand, her cool fingers brushing across his knuckles.

This is why I can't go to sleep, Michael thought. If he slept now, he might sleep until who knew when. And Michael was afraid of what he might be when he woke up.

He had to save Star. If they were going to have any life together . . . No, Michael thought, it was even more than that. If he was going to stay a human being, he had to carry her out of here. He had to save both of them.

Michael picked Star up gently, gathering her cape around her. Somehow she seemed lighter in his arms than Laddie had before. He would get her out of here easily. Michael wanted to carry her forever.

He pushed the curtain out of the way and began the long journey back to the car.

So where were the vampires?

It was creepy enough in here for them. Huge stalagmites reached raggedly toward the ceiling far above. And the jagged rocks were covered by spiderwebs and mossy vines. It was pitch black in here, too, the only light provided by Edgar and Alan's flashlight beams. Somewhere, in the distance, Sam heard the slow dripping of water.

"Where?" Edgar muttered.

"This has *gotta* be the place!" Alan agreed.

The Frogs looked at each other. Without saying another word they both turned their flashlights toward the ceiling.

Sure enough, there were the vampires.

There were four of them up there, hanging from the ceiling like something that was half human, half bat. The Lost Boys, Sam thought. The Lost Vampire Boys.

Sam swallowed. "I thought they'd be in coffins."

"That's exactly what this cave is," Edgar replied. "One great big coffin."

Edgar and Alan both began to climb one of the jagged rock walls.

"We've found them at their most vulnerable," Edgar called back.

"Easy pickings," Alan added.

"Hey!" Sam yelled at them from down below. "You just have to kill the leader!"

"How do we know which one he is?" Edgar replied. "We'll have to kill them all."

Alan turned his flashlight on the nearest vampire.

"Yeah," he called, "we'll start with the little one first. First come, first staked."

"What's that," Sam yelled up, "a little vampire humor?" He didn't think there was anything all that funny. They had to get this thing over with if they were going to save Michael. And the Frogs had said themselves that they'd never killed a vampire before.

What if something went wrong?

Edgar slid a stake out of Alan's knapsack. The Frog Brothers exchanged a final nod. Edgar positioned the stake so that its point rested over the vampire's heart.

He lifted his mallet back and drove it in with a single blow.

The vampire opened his mouth and screamed. His eyes were open too. Something poured out of the wound, something too thick and dark for blood. He kept on screaming. His scream would never end.

The vampire fell from the ceiling, hitting the cave floor with a sickening thud. The dark, thick slime gushed from around the stake, erupted from his mouth, his nose, his ears in great, bubbling gobs. The vampire's skin cracked and fell away. Sam realized the thing was decomposing right in front of him.

There were other screams overhead, shrieks of anger rather than agony. The first vampire's death howls had awakened the rest of them.

The two closest to the Frogs opened their eyes before the brothers could move.

The last vampire's eyes opened and looked straight at Sam. Sam knew this guy! He was the gang leader, David.

And then Sam knew. The gang leader must be the vampire leader.

The vampire leader growled and showed his fangs. But when he spoke, it was with David's voice.

"You're dead meat."

Thirty-one

Sam had to run faster than he had ever run before.

Edgar and Alan were right behind him.

Behind them were the vampires. It had all happened so fast. You stake one vampire, and a second later, three others are on your case.

Sam and the Frogs had run, but not before they had seen the three remaining vampires drop from the ceiling, flip around in midair, and land on their feet.

What was left of the vampire they had killed was between Sam and the tunnel out. Sam backed away from David and the others, glancing behind him at the last remains, a mound of clothes and decomposing flesh.

The mound moved.

Sam almost died. Hadn't they killed it? Would it rise again to take revenge?

The Frogs had slid down the wall to his side. Alan shone his light on the moving corpse. It was covered by rats and small, shining black beetles that quickly finished the work the Frogs had started.

The vampires leapt for them with a shriek. Sam and the others jumped over the corpse and ran for their lives.

They had to get out of the tunnel. They had to get into the light. A cold wind blew against Sam's back. He expected, with every step he took, to feel strong hands pluck him from the ground and teeth sink into his neck.

Then there was light ahead. The space above the elevator

was only a few dozen yards away. Somehow Sam managed to run even faster.

He threw himself through the hole, landing and rolling across the lobby floor. Edgar was next, then Alan. David's hands reached after them. The vampire screamed as his arms were burned in the sunlight, jerking back into the tunnel's protective darkness.

Sam and the others ran out of the cave and up the stairs. They had to get as far away from this place as they could before dark.

"Michael!" Sam yelled as they reached the top of the cliff. "Start the car!"

"We blew it, Edgar!" Alan barked behind him. "We lost it!"

"Shut up!" Edgar shouted back.

But Alan wouldn't shut. "We unraveled in the face of the enemy!"

"They pulled a mind scramble on us, man!" his brother answered. "It wasn't our fault! They opened their eyes and talked."

That, Sam thought, is what I get for taking on first-time vampire killers. We've really screwed up. The head vampire's still alive, and he knows exactly who we are and what we were trying to do. Just how are we going to get out of this one?

The Chevy was parked just ahead. Michael had parked the car so that its nose pointed straight at the cliff. They'd have to turn it around somehow to get it out of here. Sam decided he'd let his brother worry about that.

"Michael!" he called again. There was still no answer. Had something happened to him? Sam ran to the Chevy.

His brother had passed out in the back seat of the car, his feet still sticking out the window.

"Oh, great," Alan muttered. Edgar looked like he was about to say something about double-crossing vampires.

"Let's get him in the car!" Sam ordered. It was the

right approach. The Frogs did what they were told, helping Sam push Michael's feet down into the backseat.

"Now what?" Edgar asked.

Yeah, Sam thought. Now what? He had taken the initiative, it was up to him.

"I'll drive," he replied coolly.

Alan looked doubtfully into the car. "We don't ride with vampires."

"Fine!" Sam answered. "Stay here!" He ran around the car and got behind the wheel.

The Frogs looked back toward the cave. They looked at each other. They jumped in the front seat next to Sam. Sam leaned over the backseat and found the keys in Michael's pocket. He put the key in the ignition and turned. It started just as smoothly as it had the other day with Grandpa in the garage.

So far so good, Sam thought. Now what should he do next? He reached his hand behind the steering wheel to shift the car out of park.

"Come on!" Edgar yelled. "Burn rubber!"

The Frog reached his foot over and stomped down hard on the gas pedal. The Chevy took off in reverse.

Sam jammed on the brake. Tires squealed as the car rocked to a halt. The back of the Chevy was over the edge of the cliff, its back wheels just barely on the dirt.

He turned to Edgar.

"Burn rubber does not mean *warp speed*!"

That seemed to quiet the Frog Brothers down. At least for a while. And, by almost going over the cliff, the car had gotten itself pointed back toward the dirt road. Now, if Sam could just figure out how to steer this thing without going off the road, he'd be fine.

Sam reached over and turned on the radio.

Thirty-two

They were home at last. Sam jumped out of the car. His Grandpa's place had never looked so good. Sam decided he never wanted to drive again!

The ride had finally woken Michael up. He pulled Star gently from the car. Sam and the Frogs joined together to carry Laddie. They'd take them in the house, up to their rooms. They had talked it over as they drove through Santa Carla and had decided to come home by default. There was just no place else they could go.

Michael led them into the house, through the foyer, and across the front hall to the stairs. Nanook bounded out of the living room, barking for all he was worth.

Oh, no! The dog would ruin everything. Sam made a shushing noise. It didn't work.

"No, Nanook!" Sam said firmly. "Quiet! Quiet!"

It didn't work. The dog kept barking.

Edgar grunted in Nanook's direction. "Your dog knows flesh eaters when he smells 'em."

Nanook barked even louder.

"Take him outside, Sam," his brother said.

Michael was right. They had to get the dog out of the way before Grandpa came out and started asking questions. Edgar and Alan shifted around so that they took Laddie's weight between them. Sam grabbed Nanook's collar and dragged him outside. He'd have to tie the dog to his leash until he quieted down.

"Sorry, Nanook," he said as he led the dog down the

front stairs. Sam guessed there were still a few things that the dog didn't understand.

Michael led the way upstairs. He felt a lot better since his sleep in the car. His muscles seemed to be working again, and he could carry Star without too much strain. Even his ankle seemed to be feeling a little better. Maybe he was starting to get over this vampire thing.

Then it occurred to him that there might be another reason for his increasing strength: It was getting closer to nightfall.

At least Sam had gotten Nanook out of the way. Without the barking dog there was a good chance they could make it to his bedroom without being discovered. Michael didn't know how he'd explain Star and Laddie, not to mention the Frogs, if Mom or Grandpa should show up.

"Michael!"

Michael froze. He looked up at the top of the stairs. It was Grandpa.

"Do you know," Grandpa said sternly, "the rule about filling the car up with gas when you take it without askin'?"

"Uh," Michael replied. How was he going to explain all this? "No, Grandpa. . . ."

"Well, now you know." Grandpa stroked his mustache meaningfully and marched on down the hall.

He was gone. Michael remembered to breathe. Once again he led the expedition up the stairs.

Sam took the stairs two at a time. Edgar and Alan stood outside Michael's room. Sam glanced inside and saw that his brother had put both the sleepers down on his bed. He looked to the Frogs.

"Well, we blew Plan A."

Alan stared back stonily. "Time to activate Plan B."

"What's Plan B?" Sam asked.

"We don't have one yet," Edgar answered. He glanced

at his watch. "And we have two and a half hours to come up with one."

Sometimes the Frogs' military precision made Sam uneasy.

"What happens in two and a half hours?" he asked.

It was Edgar's turn to stare stonily. "The sun goes down and they'll be comin' for us."

Plan B.

Sam and the Frogs raced to the church on their bikes. They didn't have much time. The sun had sunk low enough to hit the top of the cross in the archway by the side of the church.

They ran up the steps and into the chapel. There was a christening going on up by the altar. That was too bad. It meant the holy water up there was off limits. Still, there was enough in the bowls at the back of the church to fill a couple canteens. It would have to do. The three of them worked quickly and left.

It was still taking too long. Their bikes, in the sun when they had parked them minutes ago, were covered now by long shadows.

The sun was almost down!

Plan B.

Sam ran into Max's Video. His mother was talking to a customer at the counter. Sam hurried up to them.

"Mom! Listen to me! This is very important! Santa Carla is crawling with vampires!"

His mother frowned. The customer looked at Sam and moved away. His mother took Sam's arm and led him down to the end of the counter.

"We killed one!" Sam continued rapidly. "We destroyed him. It was horrible! Edgar staked him. He was screaming and fizzing! Purple slime was gushing out of his body! And then the others woke up and said we were dead

meat!'' He paused long enough to gulp down some air.
"Mom, you gotta tell somebody!"

His mother's frown had grown even deeper.

"Sam! This isn't funny!"

"I'm not kidding!" Sam insisted. "They're coming to
the house as soon as it gets dark!" How could his mother
think this was some kind of joke? Wasn't she listening to
what he was saying?

"Stop it Sam!" his mother said in that-tone-of-voice.
"Stop it right now!"

"But, Mom—" Sam began.

"Not another word!" his mother ordered. "I don't believe you're doing this. I'm going to see Max tonight, and
you're trying to ruin it for me again."

"No, I'm not—" Sam protested.

"There's nothing wrong with Max," his mother continued. "I don't know why you don't—"

This was too much! His mother just wasn't listening!
The words exploded out of Sam's mouth.

"I'm not talking about Max! To hell with Max!"

Now all the customers in the store were looking at them.
Sam closed his eyes. What had he done?

"I'll deal with you later, young man," his mother said.

That's what he'd done. Sealed his doom. Mom would
never listen to him now. He walked out of the store.

The Frogs waited for him outside.

"We're on our own," he told them.

"Good," Alan replied.

"That's the way we like it," Edgar added.

They got back on their bikes. It was time for the next step.

Grandpa was working in the stuffed-animal room. Sam
stuck his head in the door.

"Grandpa?" he said. "The Widow Johnson called. She
said to pick her up at seven instead of eight."

Grandpa looked up from the goose he was stuffing with a frown. ''Did we have a date tonight?''

''I guess so,'' Sam replied. ''She said not to be late.''

Grandpa stood up and put his stuffing tools away. ''I'd better get cleaned up, then.'' He scratched his head as he walked hurriedly from the room.

Sam watched him go up the stairs, only the slightest bit guilty. It would be better if Grandpa wasn't around when the vampires attacked.

Plan B.

Thirty-three

Everything was ready.

Michael and Sam had locked all the doors and windows. Michael had even boarded up a couple of the windows that he thought could be broken easily. Sam and the Frogs had filled a half dozen water pistols with holy water, while the Frogs had added the rest of the stuff they had gotten from the church into a full bathtub. Sam had lined the kitchen counter with a substantial supply of garlic, while Edgar and Alan both put on camouflage makeup per instructions in a how-to article they found in *Soldier of Fortune*.

They were as ready as they were going to be. Now all they had to do was wait.

Michael looked out his bedroom window. The sun had just fallen below the horizon, and the sunset was a spectacular red. Not quite the color of blood but close enough. Michael wondered if this was the last sunset he would ever see.

Still, he felt far better now than he had all day. The night gave him strength. He was half a vampire already, and he would have to use that strength if he was to defeat David and the others.

Star groaned behind him on the bed. Michael turned around. She and the kid were both awake.

"They'll be coming for Laddie and me, won't they?" she asked.

Michael shrugged. "They'll be coming for all of us now."

He walked past the bed to the closet in the corner. He had thought of something else that they could use. He opened the door and rummaged around for a long moment. He came out carrying a hunting bow and a quiver of arrows.

Come for us now, David, Michael thought. We're as ready as we'll ever be. He didn't know, really, if his little group had any chance at all against vampires. But it was time to find out. He wanted it all to end tonight.

This should be the perfect evening. Then why was she so upset?

Lucy rang the door bell. Sam's being silly, she told herself for the twentieth time. I should forget about his stories and just have a good time.

Max opened the door and ushered her inside. He led her into the living room. It was a large space and well decorated with comfortable-looking, low-slung furniture that somehow made the place both modern and homey at the same time.

Max led her over to a side table where a bottle of wine was cooling in an ice bucket. He turned back to her. There was something boyish in his grin. It made her want to smile back.

She realized they had been standing there for a while, just looking at each other.

"Maybe," Max said at last, "this is the night where everything goes right for a change."

"I hope so," Lucy said.

Max frowned, sensing her distress.

"Something the matter?"

"No, no," Lucy replied with a little laugh. She didn't want to destroy the mood now. "Just worrying about my boys—as usual."

Max picked up a glass and poured her some wine.

"Let me tell you something about boys." He handed her the glass. "They're like weeds. They grow best when they're ignored."

Their fingers touched as Lucy accepted the glass.

"But," she added, "I thought you said they needed discipline."

"Well," Max said with a shrug. "What do I know? I'm a bachelor." He picked up a second glass, as if to pour some wine for himself, but stopped to look in Lucy's eyes.

"Lucy," he said hoarsely. "This is going to be a very special night, I promise you."

He put his glass back down and took a step away, as if to check on something in the kitchen. Lucy reached out to touch his arm. He looked back, a little startled, a little confused. He stepped back to her, and she kissed him on the lips.

Lucy had imagined this kiss for a long, long time; slow and sweet, a kiss that could last forever. She felt a warmth, deep inside her, that she hadn't felt in far too long. This night would turn out to be really special, after all.

Max led her to the sofa. They kissed again.

Thorn growled. What was that? Lucy pushed away from their embrace. She had heard a strange noise outside, like the sound of wings or the distant whispering of the wind.

Max looked at her with a frown of concern. "What's the matter, Lucy? You're so jumpy tonight."

She sighed. She might as well admit it. "It's Sam. And this crazy story. I can't get it out of my head."

Max took her hand. "Tell me."

Lucy shook her head. "If he made it up, I've got a real troubled kid on my hands. But if it's the truth—" She stopped herself mid-sentence. "*How* could it be the truth?"

"Lucy!" Max squeezed her hand tight in his. "For God's sake, tell me!"

Lucy looked at the new man in her life. She had been dealing with problems by herself far too long. Maybe Max was right. Maybe it was time she shared them.

Thirty-four

It was night. The sun was gone for good.

Sam walked into the living room. The Frogs had asked everybody to meet there for final instructions. Edgar and Alan were already there, along with Star and Laddie. Michael was still upstairs, checking to make sure everything was secure.

Alan issued everybody water pistols. He handed Edgar and Sam a few cloves of garlic besides.

Edgar waved Sam toward a seat, then began to talk.

"I think I should warn you all: It's never pretty when a vampire buys it. No two bloodsuckers ever go out the same way." He paused to see that everybody was getting this. "Some scream and yell. Some go quietly. Some explode. Some *implode*. But *all* of them will try to take you with them."

Nanook started to bark. It sounded far away.

Sam realized he had left the dog outside.

"Nanook!" he yelled, racing for the front door. "I left him tied up in the yard!"

"Don't go out there!" Edgar yelled. "Stop him!"

But Sam was already gone. He couldn't let anything happen to his dog!

Where was Sam going?

Michael ran down the stairs. He had just boarded up the trapdoor to the attic, the last thing he could think of to make the house secure. He was on his way down to meet with the others when Sam ran out the front door.

"The dog!" Star shouted to him as he reached the living room. "He went after the dog!"

"Don't follow him!" Edgar demanded. "They'll pick us off one by one."

Michael knew the Frog kid was right. They'd be easy prey for the vampires out in the yard. But Sam was his brother. Michael had gotten the kid into this thing in the first place.

He ran out the front door, after Sam.

He thought he heard wings, far overhead. He didn't look up. He only had time to run.

"Nanook!"

The dog was barking frantically. There must be vampires all over the place. And here Sam was, right out in the middle of them.

He had tied Nanook out here this afternoon, in the usual spot, just this side of Grandpa's vegetable garden. He rushed around the side of the house. Nanook was still there! The dog strained on his rope, barking at the sky.

It was hard to hear with Nanook's racket, but Sam thought he heard another sound, too, a distant whispering.

He ran to the dog.

"Come on, Nanook," he said reassuringly. "I wouldn't forget you."

The dog panted and whined for a second as he recognized Sam, then turned back to barking at the sky. Sam tried to grab his collar, but the dog was so upset that he wouldn't stand still.

"Nanook!" Sam insisted. "Just a minute. We gotta get you out of here."

The dog, startled by Sam's tone of voice, calmed down for a second before the barks resumed. Sam reached forward quickly and managed to grab the collar at last. He ran his hand down to where he had knotted the rope around the collar's metal loop.

"One second Nanook," he reassured the dog, "and we're outta here."

He tugged at the knot. It didn't want to give. Why had he tied it so tight? Then he realized that Nanook had probably tightened it with all his frantic jumping around. Well, he'd get it in a minute. It was only a simple square knot, after all. His hands slipped while he struggled with the rope. Why did his palms have to sweat at a time like this?

This knot was impossible! What happened to your cub scout training when you really needed it?

Sam paused to take a breath. The whispering was much closer now. And there was another sound, like a great rush of air, a wind from nowhere.

Nanook went wild.

Maybe, Michael thought, I should have slammed the door behind me. He risked a look behind him. Star, Laddie, and the Frogs stood in the doorway, watching him.

His foot hit a rock in the lawn, and he almost stumbled. Michael swore. His ankle felt better. He didn't want to twist it all over again. He kept his eyes on Sam and the dog.

Nanook was still on his rope. Sam was trying to untie the knot at the dog's collar. The other end was tied around a tree by the garden.

He ran up by Sam and grabbed Nanook's collar. The knot was hopeless, pulled so tight that it felt more like stone than rope.

Michael undid the dog's collar.

Sam looked up and saw the vampire. The creature was high above them in the sky. But it was coming fast.

Sam screamed.

Michael had Nanook free! He grabbed Sam's arm and they ran, Nanook by their side. The Frogs yelled at them to hurry up as they rounded the corner of the house. Sam could hear the whispering behind them.

They were calling Michael's name.

Sam risked a look back. Oh, shit! The vampire flew over the tree where Nanook had been tied. The thing was almost on top of them!

They ran for the doorway. The vampire screamed behind them. Sam was sure he could feel the thing's cold breath on the back of his neck. Star screamed for them to hurry. Laddie screamed, "Watch out!"

They were through the door. The Frogs slammed it shut. Something banged heavily against the other side.

Michael tried to catch his breath. He nodded to the Frogs.

"Hide Star and Laddie upstairs," he told them after a moment.

The Frogs saluted and led the other two up to Michael's bedroom.

Michael looked at Sam. They were both too tired to talk. After what happened, they needed a minute to get their act together.

There was a clumping noise in the living room.

Nanook turned and growled.

Thirty-five

The fireplace exploded.

Dwayne stood there, or something that had once been Dwayne. He looked thinner than before, with long, clawlike fingernails on his hands. His face, though, had changed even more. His brows were heavier, bestial, and his eyes glowed red from within. The bottom half of his face seemed to be nothing but mouth; a mouth filled with sharpened teeth.

Here, at last, was a real vampire, Michael thought. This is what I will become.

Dwayne leapt from the fireplace with a howl. Both Sam and Michael jumped back. But Dwayne had leapt above them to grab the chandelier that hung from the middle of the ceiling. The creature's feet lashed out, kicking first Sam, then Michael, to the floor.

Michael looked up. The chandelier was falling.

Then the lights went out.

She had started to hope.

The Frog Brothers, Edgar and Alan, led Star and Laddie up the stairs; real wooden stairs, with a real banister on the side.

Michael had taken her out of the cave, away from the Lost Boys. But more than that, he had brought her home, to a real house with a real yard, full of all those common, everyday things. Things she had grown up with and now had almost forgotten. She never realized how much she missed all those ordinary, everyday things until she thought she could never have them again.

David had told her to forget about her past, about the day-to-day world that she could no longer be a part of. She was one of them now, part of a wonderful new life that would last forever. She had believed him too. There was no part of the everyday world she wanted to keep. Her mother had almost killed her. Her father wished she had never been born. There had been nothing to do but run, to find something new. David had offered her that something, a new world. She would have kept on believing in that new world, too, if she hadn't met Michael.

Michael had given her hope. With him she thought it really might be possible to start fresh, in the daylight, and be a human being again. She wanted to make that change. Now David and the others were here, looking to take her and Laddie back.

She wouldn't let that happen. Even if it meant hurting David and the others, she had found the place where she was going to stay.

Edgar and Alan hurried both Star and Laddie into the upstairs bedroom. She told Laddie to get under the bed. Maybe that way he wouldn't have to see all the terrible things that were going to happen. Edgar looked in the closet and the bathroom, then double-checked the locks on the windows. Everything seemed locked, secure.

Something crashed downstairs. The vampires must have gotten in! Alan grabbed the bedroom door and slammed it shut.

There was a vampire behind the door. It walked toward them, its mouth filled with grinning fangs.

Laddie rolled under the bed.

Everybody else screamed.

Sam knew there was a light around here someplace. He

crawled across the floor, expecting at any second to run into a vampire foot, or something even worse.

His hand found the cold metal of the floor lamp. It had fallen on its side. He got to his knees as quietly as possible, feeling along the length of the lamp until he found the switch. He turned on the light.

Michael was on the floor nearby. He wasn't moving. The vampire must have knocked him out.

Where was the vampire? Sam couldn't see him anywhere. It was too quiet. The thing must be hiding somewhere in the shadows.

Sam crawled over to his unconscious brother. He had to get Michael out of here before the vampire did something worse. He shook his brother's shoulder.

"Wake up, Michael!" Sam yelled. "Please?" His brother really picked the worst times to pass out.

Sam heard a noise overhead.

Sam looked up. The thing pushed away from the ceiling, straight for him. It grabbed Sam's shoulders before he could move, lifting him completely off the floor. Sam could feel the thing's icy breath as its face snaked down to reach his neck.

Sam reached into his belt and grabbed his water pistol. He twisted around and squirted the holy water into the vampire's face. The creature shrieked, releasing Sam to cover his burning face.

Sam was falling. He saw the banister below him, coming up fast. Sam grabbed at the slippery wood as he fell to one side, landing on the couch below.

Across the room, Michael rolled over and groaned.

Sam looked up. The vampire was coming again. He had to get out of here.

The bloodsucker screamed as it swept down, mouth opened wide.

Sam jumped from the couch. How do you get away from something that flies?

*   *.   *

It was Paul. The vampire was Paul. It took Star a moment to realize that. Out of all the Lost Boys, Paul had probably been the kindest to her. Now he wasn't even human.

Paul walked toward them across the room. The Frogs had each grabbed a wooden stake from a pack they had brought with them. They held them out toward Paul, waving them in his face as if they were going to challenge the vampire to a sword fight. Paul swatted them aside and laughed. When he laughed, all Star could see were his long, pointed fangs.

There was a noise under the bed.

"Laddie!" Star whispered. "Stay under there!"

She didn't want him seeing this. But she realized now that there was another reason she had hidden him, too; that maybe, just maybe, even if the vampires took her back, they might forget about Laddie and leave him behind.

"Holy water!" Edgar yelled.

The Frogs grabbed their water pistols from where they had tucked them in the tops of their pants. They shot two streams at the approaching vampire.

The water sizzled where it hit Paul. It ran off his skin in pale, white rivulets, as if it were melting his skin and was no longer just water but liquid flesh.

Paul laughed and kept on coming.

There was a real banging under the bed. What was Laddie doing? She had to calm the boy down.

"Laddie!" Star pleaded. "Everything will be all right. Just stay there, please?"

Paul was almost on top of them.

"You're mine," he hissed at the Frog Brothers. "You killed Marco!"

"Oh, yeah?" Edgar yelled back. "Well, you're next!"

Paul shook his head.

"*You're* next."

He stepped toward the Frogs. Edgar and Alan ran into the bathroom. Paul stopped at the door and laughed. From her position by the bed Star could see the Frogs cowering by a bathtub filled with maybe a hundred cloves of garlic floating on the surface.

"Garlic don't work, boys!" Paul laughed again as he stepped into the bathroom.

"Then try a little holy water, death breath!" Edgar cupped a handful of bathwater and threw it at Paul's face. The vampire drew back, wisps of smoke rising from its sizzling flesh. Paul growled and stepped purposefully toward the Frog Brothers.

The hallway door slammed open. Claws clacked across the hardwood floor. The vampire spun around to deal with the new threat.

It was the dog, Star realized. Sam's dog, Nanook.

It leapt for Paul with a growl.

Paul twisted around to grapple with the animal, but the dog was too fast. Nanook's sudden weight pushed Paul back into the bathroom.

There was a splash. Star ran to the door. Paul had fallen into the full bathtub.

Paul shrieked and kicked, a look of real terror on his face. The water began to bubble, and his screams grew higher, as if parts of him were being ripped away.

The water turned to foam, first boiling up from the tub, then shooting into the air like a geyser. Paul disappeared beneath the spray, but Star could still hear his screams, rising higher and higher, as if they came from some tortured animal, and then higher still but fainter, as if they came from some flying thing, far away and on the edge of death.

The screams stopped. The bubbling mess in the tub was no longer clear, but something between gray and pink. It started to drain away. Star thought she caught a final glimpse of Paul's face, and then the water was gone.

The water pipes groaned.

"Watch out!" Edgar cried.

The sink and toilet exploded, vomiting forth the grayish-pink waste. Star leapt back as the liquid sprayed across the room. She heard explosions in other parts of the house, as if every pipe in the place had burst.

But Paul was gone. Star walked out into the hallway, her legs shaking beneath her, thankful that there was nothing at all in her stomach.

The vampire's claws were coming for his eyes! Sam twisted away and saw Michael trying to fit an arrow into his bow. He looked up, trying to keep his hands steady enough to fire.

"Sam!" Michael yelled. "Duck!"

The vampire leapt over Sam, jumping on top of Michael. The bow and arrow flew out of Michael's grip and skittered across the floor to the base of the stuffed mountain lion.

The vampire's hands were around his brother's neck. Sam ran across the room, scooping up first the arrow, then the bow. What worked for his brother could just work for him. He fitted the arrow like he had been taught in junior-high archery practice, leaning against the mountain lion for support.

All right, you bloodsucker, Sam thought.

Michael's flailing fists managed to drive the vampire up to a sitting position. Michael pulled the claws from his neck, gasping for breath.

"Surprise!" Sam shouted.

The vampire looked up. Sam let the arrow fly.

The bloodsucker leapt high in the air. The arrow flew past it to imbed itself in the wall.

The vampire laughed. "You missed, sucker!"

But Sam had already fitted another arrow into the bow. "Only once, sucker!" He let it fly as the vampire came for him.

The vampire roared as the arrow sliced through his neck. The force of the arrow threw the creature back against the stereo, hard. Music blasted from the speakers, heavy-metal rock and roll. The arrowhead had slashed right through the power switch. Electricity surged through the vampire, roared through the speakers as the whole system short-circuited, the creature bursting apart like a ripe melon with the final surge of energy.

The stereo amplifier shot off a few more sparks before it died. On the floor below, what little was left of the vampire fizzled and smoked.

Sam whistled softly.

"Death by stereo."

They had just killed Dwayne.

Star stood in the hallway and tried to get her thoughts together. So much was happening so fast.

They were killing the Lost Boys. In a way they had been her family. She had been with them for a couple weeks, ever since she had run away to Santa Carla. But she had never seen them as vampires. For some reason they had hidden it from her. She realized she had never known their true selves, ony their human remains.

Still, she didn't like to see them die. She wished there was some other way. But she was beginning to realize that there wasn't. If the vampires didn't die, she would become one of them.

And that was something she never wanted to happen.

She leaned against the doorway, half in the bedroom, half in the hall. She just wished the whole thing would be over.

Edgar and Alan walked back in the bedroom, fresh from inspecting the vampire remains in the bath.

Edgar laughed. "See that sucker burn?"

Alan reached out his hand and slapped his brother's palm.

"We totally annihilated his night-stalkin' ass!"

They collapsed on the bed where they had stored their final canteen of holy water.

Edgar started to refill his water pistol.

"Death to all vampires!"

"Maximum body count!" Alan agreed with a nod.

"We are awesome monster bashers!" Edgar added.

"The meanest!"

"The baddest!"

They swung their arms over their heads, slapping each other's palms once again.

The bed began to shake.

"Laddie?" Star whispered. Something was wrong!

The mattress bulged between the Frogs. It heaved upward, ripping in two. Pieces of sheet and mattress flew through the air.

Laddie stood between Alan and Edgar, where the mattress once had been.

He had turned into a vampire.

Thirty-six

The Frogs jumped from the bed with a yell.

Laddie ripped what was left of the mattress into tiny shreds. Edgar and Alan had retreated into the corner. Laddie smiled and followed them. He no longer looked like an eleven-year-old boy. He was a beast of the night, stalking its prey.

Star rushed into the room. She stepped between the vampire and the Frogs.

"Laddie!" she commanded. "*No!*"

They heard screams coming from upstairs.

Sam and Michael looked at each other, then ran up the stairs, Sam in the lead. The other vampires must be attacking Star and the others. Michael held on to his bow and arrow, ready to pierce another one of the creatures through the heart.

Sam ran into the bedroom. Michael slowed as he reached the top of the stairs. He had to give himself time to fit the arrow into the bow.

David swung down in front of him, upside down, hanging from a rafter. He pushed Michael, hard.

Michael fell down the stairs.

What was that?

Sam had rushed into the room to see Star standing between the Frog Brothers and a vampire. But the vampire was changing in front of him: the fangs receded; the face softened.

The vampire was Laddie.

Then the noise came from the hallway. Sam turned around to see his brother falling down the stairs. David jumped down from the rafter into the hall. He glanced at Sam and laughed.

The bedroom door slammed shut, all by itself.

Michael got up from where he had fallen. His shoulder was sore—he had probably bruised it badly—but nothing seemed to be broken. His hands were empty. He had lost the bow and arrow in the fall.

David stood at the top of the stairs. He regarded Michael, hands on hips, the vampire lord.

"Give up, Michael!" he called. "You're one of us. Don't you understand that?" He put out his hands as he took a step down the stairs. "You're one of us."

"No!" Michael yelled back to him. He would not be one of them. He looked around frantically, searching for a weapon.

"Don't make me kill you, Michael!" David called.

Michael raised his fists, ready to fight off the vampire any way he could.

But David launched himself away from the stairs to fly just below the ceiling. He swooped down behind Michael, his claws extended. Michael heard his shirt rip. He cried out as he felt searing pain along his back.

David was gone again. Michael reached his hand around to feel his back. His ribs were wet with blood.

He braced himself, standing despite the pain, looking around for the next attack. David was too fast. He didn't know how he could fight him. David would draw blood every time.

This time David flew straight down toward him. Michael dropped down, hoping to avoid the claws, looking for something he could use as a shield.

David's claws ripped open Michael's shirt sleeve. He

felt blood trickle down his arm. The pain came next, now all the way across his shoulder to his spine. If Michael couldn't find some way to stop this, the vampire was going to win. David would attack again and again, shredding away pieces of Michael until the wounds drained every last bit of strength.

Michael took a deep breath. He wasn't going to let this happen. He could feel his heart beating hard, the blood pulsing against his temples. David was not going to win. He jumped for the vampire.

Michael realized he was flying.

David's grinning face was in front of him. "He flies!" The vampire started to laugh. "And now he dies!"

His claws dug into Michael's shoulders. Michael found himself being dragged swiftly and painfully through the air.

The pounding in his head was even greater. Michael knew what he was. He knew what he needed. David was not going to win! Michael spun around, ripping his shoulders from David's grasp. He shoved David back across the room, toward the pair of deer heads on the far wall, toward the antlers, just right for impaling a vampire.

He would win. He would kill David, no matter what it took. He felt the rhythm of his blood pounding in his veins. With every beat he was growing stronger.

With every beat he was becoming more and more a vampire.

Thirty-seven

He pushed David toward the antlers. David tried to jerk away and barely managed to avoid the jagged horns. Michael slammed David against the wall, a deer head on either side. He would beat David into the ground. He would tear him into little pieces. And then?

Michael stopped, tried to breathe, tried to think. What was he doing? His anger was getting the better of him. It was turning him into something he didn't want to be.

David roared and pushed Michael away, sending him spinning through the air. David was on top of him again, and the two of them wrestled in the air. David's claws ripped open his shirtfront and gouged the skin on his chest. Michael knew then that he couldn't weaken. Not again. If he did, he was dead.

Michael saw another wall, coming up fast. They had tumbled through the air until they had crossed the entire living room, hovering just outside Grandpa's study.

David pushed again, trying to force Michael into the room in front of him. Michael grabbed the door frame instead, right above the top of the door, and shoved himself back at David. He'd push him back to the antlers again. And this time he wouldn't weaken.

"Stop fighting me, Michael!" David growled. "I don't want to kill you." He paused and almost smiled. "Join us."

Michael shook his head. He would die before he became a vampire. "Never!"

David's smile was gone. "It's too late, Michael. My blood is in your veins."

So it was David's blood that he drank? The thought of that night in the cave, and what they had done to him, made Michael even angrier.

David's blood was in him? So what?

"So is my blood." Michael spat the words back at the vampire.

And David attacked.

He pulled Michael's arms and pushed at his legs. Michael still wasn't used to this flying thing. David had gotten him off-balance. Michael fell back into the taxidermy room.

David dived into the room after him. He looked around the cluttered shelves and laughed. Michael knew what he was thinking. This place was filled with knives, mallets, sharpened teeth, and antlers. So many different ways to kill somebody.

Maybe, Michael thought, there would be some way to kill a vampire.

David was on him again, slashing and tearing. This time, though, Michael didn't struggle. Instead he pushed himself toward David, throwing him off-balance. Michael spun around, throwing David across the room. He needed a chance to think, to plan what he could do next.

David twisted away, out of control. He screamed as he flew toward a huge set of antlers that sat on Grandpa's desk. The antlers sliced through the vampire as if David didn't have a bone in his body. Smoke rose from the half dozen places where the antlers had pierced his body, followed by dark slime bubbling from the wounds. White light seemed to surround him.

Cautiously Michael settled to the ground and stepped closer to the dying vampire. If David had won, he realized, this was what would have happened to him.

David was changing.

He was surrounded now by the white light. And he no longer looked like a vampire. In fact, he didn't even look like a Lost Boy. He just looked like another teenager. Another teenager, just like Michael.

Headlights swept across the room. Michael heard a car pull up, and a pair of car doors slam, followed by running feet. Someone was coming toward the house.

Michael realized that he hadn't changed. He was still a vampire.

Thirty-eight

Star walked into the room, followed by the Frogs and Sam. All of them saw David's corpse.

"Get away," Michael said hoarsely. He had trouble talking, now that he had changed. Star walked toward him, worry on her face. How could she feel anything after what he had become?

His brother followed her. "Sam," Michael croaked urgently, "get away!"

Like usual, Sam didn't pay any attention to what his brother said.

"Michael?" he asked as he walked closer. "What's wrong?"

Michael backed away, into the shadow-filled corner.

"I said get away!"

"What's the big deal?" Edgar asked. "You destroyed the head vampire. It's all over."

That was just it. Couldn't they tell? Couldn't they see what had happened to him?

Michael shook his head. "Nothing's changed."

"He's right." Star looked very afraid. "I don't feel any different, either."

Edgar looked from Star to Michael and back again.

"Then there's still one more," he added softly.

Michael heard the sound of a key in the front door.

What could he do now?

Lucy unlocked the front door and let Max into the house. She hoped they weren't too late! After the things

Max had told her about Santa Carla, she couldn't get here fast enough.

Her heart sank as she looked inside. The entire place was a shambles. What had happened here? Where were her children?

"Michael!" she called.

Max ran in front of her, across the living room to her father's study. Lucy hurried to follow.

Sam came out of the room, followed by the Frog Brothers. Max only glanced at them as he passed.

"Hi, Mom," Sam ventured.

"Sam!" A wave of relief rushed through her. She was so glad to see him! "What happened here? Where's Michael?"

"Oh, that." Sam scuffed his foot across the debris-laden floor. "Uh—that is—you see—we had to kill a few vampires."

Max cursed as he walked into their grandfather's study.

Michael and Star held each other, hiding in the shadows at the back of the room. Max walked up to David's corpse, his mouth opened slightly with surprise. Michael didn't dare breathe. He didn't want anyone finding him; not the way he was now. How could his mother or her boyfriend understand? How could anyone understand?

Star held him close as Max turned away from David's body. He swore again as he walked from the room.

They were alone again. Cautiously Michael pulled Star with him out of the shadows. Maybe they could sneak past his mother and Max when they were exploring some other part of the house. There had to be some way out of this.

Didn't there?

Her son was talking nonsense again. Lucy walked past Sam into the decimated living room. Max walked out of Grandpa's taxidermy room to meet her.

"I'm sorry, Lucy," Max said with a frown. "This is all my fault. David and my boys misbehaved. I told you the boys needed a mother."

She stared back at Max. Wasn't anybody making any sense?

"Max, what are you talking about?"

Sam walked up beside her.

"I knew it," her son said with finality. "You're the head vampire."

The Frog Brothers joined them, one to either side of her.

She was going to stop this nonsense right now.

"Sam," she commanded, "don't start this again."

"You're the secret that David was protecting."

Lucy looked up. The voice belonged to a teenage girl who had just walked out of the taxidermy room. Lucy realized it was the girl whom Michael had been seeing.

And Max nodded at her with a sad smile.

"But you passed the test!" Alan exclaimed.

Max's smile widened.

"Never invite a vampire into your house, you silly boy. It renders you powerless."

Sam turned to Edgar with a scowl. "Did you know that?"

"Uh—" Edgar replied hesitantly, as if he didn't know it at all. "Of course. Uh—everyone knows that."

This was impossible. Just what was going on here?

"Has everyone gone crazy?" Lucy demanded. "What's the matter with all of you?"

Max turned to her.

"It was you I was after all along, Lucy."

He took a step toward her. She took a step away.

"What?" Lucy asked. Maybe she didn't want to know what was going on, after all.

"I knew!" Max continued. "I knew that if I could get Sam and Michael into the family, there was no way you could say no."

Lucy looked around. She'd had enough of this foolishness. "Where's Michael?" she demanded.

But Max was still coming toward her. "It was all going to be so perfect, Lucy. Just like one big happy family." He pointed at Sam. "Your boys—"

He turned away and pointed into the taxidermy room.

"—and my boys."

Lucy looked where Max pointed. She gasped. There, on her father's desk, was a dead body. For one horrible second she thought it was Michael, but the hair and clothes were wrong. She couldn't see the face. What had happened here?

"Great!" Edgar yelled. Lucy realized he had a knife in his hand. "The bloodsucking Brady Bunch!"

Had the whole world gone crazy?

Max turned back around. There was something wrong with his face. His eyebrows were growing, his cheekbones tightening, his whole face changing as Lucy watched.

"But I still want you, Lucy." When he spoke, she could see his fangs. His body was still changing, his back hunching over, his arms growing long and gnarled. He didn't look at all like Max anymore. It was like he had gotten old, incredibly old, but incredibly powerful as well. Muscles rippled beneath his pallid skin as he advanced on Lucy.

"I want you. I haven't changed my mind about that."

Everyone screamed, Lucy's voice joining the others.

Max reached out a hand for Lucy, a twisted thing with long nails that looked more like a claw.

There was a noise behind him. Michael walked out of the taxidermy room. But Michael had changed too. He looked like Max!

Michael growled at the vampire. "I didn't invite you this time, Max."

Max spun around to face him.

The vampire laughed.

*   *   *

Michael had to confront Max. He couldn't hide anymore. Not now. He would save his mother. Somehow he would save her!

The thing that had been Max opened its mouth and roared. The sound was like the screams of a thousand lost souls, or a thousand times a thousand, everyone the vampire had ever drained of blood crying out their death agonies. It rushed over them like a gale, forcing everything to the floor. Michael looked around him. Star, the Frogs, his mother, Sam—all of them were held, writhing on the ground, holding their ears against the noise.

The roar threatened to force Michael to his knees. The screams sounded like his own screams as the demon wind threatened to shred the skin from his body.

Michael would not kneel. He would not fall down and cower. He stood against the force of the sound and jumped for Max.

The creature grabbed Michael and threw him over its head, like someone might throw away an empty bottle. Michael saw the top of the stairs coming fast. He was headed straight for the banister!

Lucy looked up. The hellish noise was gone. Then she saw Max lift Michael over his head and throw him toward the ceiling.

Her son's body flailed like a rag doll as it arced across the room, smashing against the banister at the top of the stairs, then hitting the wall beyond. Michael fell to the floor.

"Michael!" Lucy called. Her son didn't move.

The thing that had been Max turned to her and smiled.

Michael's girlfriend had found a bow and arrow someplace. She hastily tried to notch the arrow and draw back the bow. Max rushed forward and tossed her aside before she could finish, then brushed aside the Frog Brothers as if they were flies. He turned to Lucy once again.

Sam stepped in front of her.

"Don't you touch my mother."

"Sam!" Lucy yelled. "No!"

But her son was already rushing headlong toward the vampire. Max grabbed the boy and twisted him around, holding the child's head tight in the crook of his arm.

The vampire held his free hand out to her.

"Don't fight, Lucy," he said in his dry, dead whisper. "It's so much better if you don't fight."

"Mom! Mom!" shrieked Sam, still held in Max's headlock. "Don't do it, Mom! Don't do it!"

Max tightened his grip on the boy. Lucy shivered. What else could she do?

She reached out and took Max's hand. She didn't want to look at him but couldn't pull her eyes away.

What had he become? His fangs hung down below his jaw; his eyes glowed yellow from within; his skin was so dry and white that if you touched it, it might turn to dust. He didn't just look like a vampire. He no longer looked human.

"Sam—" she began, but whatever she was going to say fled as she looked up to see the vampire's fangs descending toward her neck.

Then she saw something else, over Max's shoulder. Taillights backing rapidly toward the house.

It was a truck. Grandpa's truck.

"Jump, Mom!" Sam was at her side, pulling her away. The driver beeped the horn.

The truck played "La Cucaracha."

"La Cucaracha?"

Michael opened his eyes and pushed himself up to his knees. He looked back downstairs.

The vampire held his mother in its arms. But Sam pulled her away as Grandpa's truck burst through the front double doors. Grandpa must have loaded three dozen sharpened fence posts on the back of the truck, and they were all headed straight for Max!

The vampire turned around and saw the stakes. He glanced around quickly, looking for the best escape. He would get away!

Not if Michael could help it.

He leapt from the landing where he had fallen, aimed straight for Max's back.

The vampire saw him. He turned, ready to jump the other way.

But the truck was on top of him, braking suddenly. A pair of stakes flew from the flatbed, piercing the creature's chest as if he were hollow inside.

Michael jumped clear as Max tumbled back into the fireplace. Michael fell to the floor, exhausted.

Max roared in agony, the final cry of his thousand souls. He pulled weakly at the stake in his chest for an instant. Then flames shot forth from the wound, and the roar of his voice was lost beneath the sound of a great wind that seemed to rush out from within the vampire. Max's face and hands grew older and older still as Michael watched, the skin wrinkling and cracking, then falling to dust. The skin flaked away, then the bones, then the dried things inside the bones. And as his body fell away, bright light, red and orange like the flames, erupted from somewhere inside him to brightly light the room.

Then, all at once, the light turned to flame, and Max's body was engulfed.

The room was filled with blinding light. They heard Max scream a final time.

A fireball erupted from the fireplace, streaking above them for only an instant until it was extinguished in midair. A great cloud of soot blasted forth from the chimney, covering them all with ashes. The fireplace caved in with a final roar.

Then silence.

Star started to cry. "It's—over," she managed between sobs.

Edgar and Alan looked at each other. "Mission accomplished!" they chorused.

Grandpa had opened the door of the truck, brushing himself off and coughing at the soot. Laddie walked down the stairs.

"Star!" he called. "Star!"

"Laddie!" Star opened her arms to give him a hug.

Michael looked around. "Is everybody okay?"

His mother shook her head.

"Oh, Michael!"

Sam and Michael both went to give their mother a hug.

"Oh, my sons!" she added.

Edgar turned to his brother Frog. "How much do you think we should charge them for this?"

Alan took a moment to consider as Grandpa got down from the truck and walked to the kitchen.

"Dad?" their mother asked. But Grandpa didn't answer, instead walking straight for the refrigerator.

"Dad?" she asked again. "Are you all right?"

He opened the refrigerator, took out a root beer, twisted off the screw top, and took a gulp that drained half the bottle.

"Aaaahhh," he said at last. He turned to face the others.

"That's one thing about livin' in Santa Carla that I never could stomach." He pulled distractedly at his mustache. "All the damn vampires."

Epilogue

So that's how me and my daughter and my two grandsons got rid of the vampires in Santa Carla. At least, those vampires we know about.

After that things pretty much returned to normal. We fixed up the house, Lucy got a new job, Michael went back to school. Star did, too, after she found a place to stay at the Widow Johnson's. Laddie remembered where his parents lived. And Sam decided he wanted to learn to stuff animals.

But there's one little piece of the story I haven't told you about. Didn't know it myself until Michael and Star took Lucy and me on a tour of the Lost Boys' cave.

It's quite a place. A good piece of a hotel just fell into the earth, back about a hundred years ago. They built things to last in those days, so most of it's still there. Pretty impressive. Might make a good tourist attraction someday, if we let anybody know about it.

But it's what's behind the hotel that's really spooky. That place where all the Lost Boys slept is only the beginnings of the cave. Those tunnels seem to go on forever, maybe even all the way back into Santa Carla. And the noises that come out of there? My daughter insists it's just gotta be the wind. Sam says it's probably some sort of animal.

But nobody knows for sure. So you'll excuse us if we

only visit the hotel during the daylight. And we haven't quite gotten the gumption to go back there and check those noises out.

Would you?